THE DEATH OF VENUS

BY JOSEPH WILSON

The birth of Venus

An ultra marine star burns above, casting deep unnatural shadows across the faces of the demons dancing around, giving the glow of a room of drowning people flailing for life. The star switches to a deep burgundy burning below the stage, casting a demonic gory light across the faces, distorted by shadows cast from a new source. And in a second a new emerald star takes stage above, showering shades of radiation down onto the room, projecting a putrid plague around me. Amongst the crowds she strides towards me, dancing and swaying, tall and slender with a stream of silk ginger hair holding it's burning colour in the ever changing hues of the room.

"Oh come on Patrick you're barely dancing." She calls to me over the intrusive thudding shaking the room. She laughs as she says this, but with a dry humourless tone and disgust in her eyes.

"I can't hear the music." I joke far too quietly. It's lost on her and she withdraws back into the ocean of burning toxic faces.

Having finally reached my tolerance for Natalie and the repetitive soulless music being blasted too loud, I decide to take my leave to the smoking area for quiet, and ironically, some fresh air. The headliner is playing now so I'm guessing all other areas of the club will be vacant. On my way up stairs I'm forced to squeeze past a couple ignoring the world for their own passion. I uncomfortably shimmy past them on up the stairs and I hear the girl giggling behind me. Bitch. I ascend to the upper floor of the club and breeze across a mostly empty dance floor to a hall leading down unto salvation. The walls are covered in torn paper, worn sharpie, and stains I'd like to ignore. This grimy hall of infamy perfectly encapsulates why I hate these places, there's nothing pleasant to be found. I don't understand Natalie's goal, just the other day she never wanted to see me again, and yet tonight I've been dragged out to a club and grinded on as she drunkenly recounts "the good times".

There were some really good times.

There were also some really bad times.

Recently the bad has outweighed the good for which I blame her new job. She blamed me, as I don't share her view we haven't spoken much for close to a week.

I finally exit out to the smoking area, as the door swings open I feel a refreshing icy wave of cold air wash over me, a welcome change from the stuffy lack of air downstairs. I take a few seconds to close my eyes and focus on how I physically feel to avoid how I mentally feel, a much needed detox. I appreciate the crisp December air in my lungs before reopening my eyes to avoid getting too dizzy from the liqueur flowing through my system.

I start making my way to the seats in the designated smoking part of the balcony to find 1 broken and the other 3 taken up by the slumped figure of a girl sprawled across them face down and unmoving. I pull a cigarette from my pack regardless, keeping a cautious eye. She's wearing an oversized silver bomber jacket that's made it's way up to cover her head so I can't tell if she's awake or even breathing. I gently nudge her shoulder with my lighter to no avail, so I shake her shoulder slightly and say "Hello." To which she shoots up and shouts "WHAT?" back.

I recognise her instantly and recoil. No more than 40 minutes ago this girl started an argument with me out of the blue inside. Luckily with the music being so loud I didn't have to hear a word she said, but I could infer from her aggressive facial expressions and pointing finger she was pissed. I have no idea why she was trying to shout at me then and I don't want to deal with it now. She sits up haphazardly looking at my face with a great deal of confusion.

Her hair is a curly wild mess dyed vibrant purple with no visible roots, her lips are the same shade of purple, while her eye make up, despite now being very smeared, is a complementary shade of dark blue. Beneath the oversized bomber jacket she's wearing a rich red velvet top that only really covers her chest along with a skirt and fishnets. An excellent choice for a breezy night in December.

"Aren't you the guy from earlier? Oh god leave me alone." She says, lying back down.

Ok works for me, so I turn to walk off.

"Wait!" she calls out behind me, I reluctantly turn to look at her, still saying nothing.

"Why did you come out here?" she asks wearily.

I put my cigarette in my mouth, "To smoke" I say lighting it and turning to walk to the other side of the balcony.

"Then why did you touch me a second ago?" she continues

"You looked dead and in my way, but that's fine if you're ok you can lie there I'm going over here as far away as I can". Before I'm able to get away however, she speaks again, this time in an accusing tone, "Or you saw me come out here and followed me and then checked on me for an excuse to talk to me. That's it isn't it?? Spying up a vulnerable girl who rejected you earlier in the night"

Lord help me, this can't be real "I haven't spoken to you before so what were you rejecting?"

"The way you danced was suggestive." she declares "You know you were trying to get my attention."

"I assure you I have no interest in crazy, self absorbed types like you." I lie

She sits back up on the seats and mutters "You're just another old man coming after a poor young girl, creep."

My gut lurches and I drop my cigarette as I feel my body tense up. The drumbeat of my heart speeds up as I feel the approaching hoard of thoughts and feelings that often carry with it a panic attack. I focus on my breathing and refocusing my mind. Eye's burning with the pain I just held back I glower at her and repeat my mantra "I'm only 21, I'm still young and have much to look forward to."

The sides of her mouth begin to raise but she quickly hides it by speaking again "Ugh gross I'm only like 18."

"That explains the immaturity." I mean to say only in my head, but let slip. With this I pull my pack of cigarettes back out and start to walk away, when yet again she calls out.

"So you're just going to leave me as well? Alone and suffering?"

Don't fall for it don't fall for it

"Suffering with what?"

"A broken heart."

I fell for it, I fucking fell for it.

"Me too kid." I say, walking off swiftly.

I prop myself at the far end of the balcony overlooking downtown. The view really is breath-taking, The whole town is lit up for Christmas with houses and business engulfed in the glowing decor. I can see the Christmas market where I work, which from so far away looks beautiful. An array of colourful lights dancing from red to green and back, illuminating the little wooden huts from alternating angles. Moments like this are the closest I'll come to believing there's magic in this city. This dark dismal shit pit inflates with wonder each December. It's all good appreciating it now, but tomorrow I know I'll be back down there, trapped in my wooden box, hating everything. I focus on a flickering snowman stuck to a building in the distance, pondering as to whether the display was intentional or a fault. Can accidental beauty have merit.

"Ex-cuse me." I hear the voice come from behind me, sarcasm already present in her tone. I flick what's left of my cigarette into the night and turn around as I hear her speak again, this time closer and with aggression in her voice. "Hey!" She calls as I turn and find her only a few feet away. "I was just going inside." I say, desperate to avoid anymore of this.

"It's ok" she replies, "I've decided to give you another chance."

I'm left dumbfounded, I didn't think she could make less sense but she keeps on surprising me. "Another chance at what?" I ask, metaphorically tip toeing to avoid any more sudden moods.

"With me, since you made such a poor first impression twice, I thought I'd give you a 3rd shot at it." She grins at me, a big wide smile, I don't smile back.

"I don't want to talk to you." I say

She pulls an overly expressive face, widening her eyes and mouth in a comical fashion "Well how rude, I just told you how hurt I'm feeling and in my pain still find the courage to offer you a 3rd chance to get to know me, and you so coldly shoot me down! Do you know who I am Hun?" Throughout this monologue she's wildly waving her arms about to emphasise points. I appreciate the performance somewhat, it's entertaining and less annoying than everything that came before.

"I don't know who you are." I reply, keeping an uninterested tone.

"Neither do I, let's find out together!" She jokingly punches the air and I think my facade may have broke slightly as she says "See knew you weren't so tough."

Not wanting to cave in to this sudden change in her personality I say "I was just going inside I don't want to keep people waiting."

She feigns an expression of concern and says "Oh you best hurry buddy, I know I'd miss you if I was people."

I can't tell if she's mocking "By people I mean friends." I clarify

"Duh!" she says, before quickly changing tone, "Maybe you can introduce me?" She uses her hands to frame her face and adopts a pose.

I pull the corners of my mouth back down and clear my throat, "I don't think my girlfriend would be too happy."

Her hands drop.

"Oh. You didn't look like you had one inside, is it the blonde one with the pigtails?"

"No. The ginger girl."

"Oh I'm sorry." Her eyes double in size but she's no longer looking at me, instead just past me. "It's ok, you didn't know."

Her eyes come back to me "I meant that she was ginger." I finally break and laugh.

She doesn't laugh. Her tone now hollow and humourless she speaks again "I am actually sorry though…"

"For your odd behaviour?" I chuckle, having apparently lost against her charm.

"No I am who I am, for that I'm unapologetic."

"I thought you didn't know who you were?"

"Yeah shut up, I'll stop feeling sorry for you."

"why do you feel sorry for me?"

She hesitantly points over the edge of the balcony "Is that her?" I follow the direction of her finger down to the street below.

My stomach erupts, the molten pain spews all over my body. And then I spew all over their bodies. Nat and her workmate Jason stop kissing on the curb. Nat screams. I stumble and almost fall but a hand grabs me and pulls me back up. This enigmatic girl is alternating between saying "Oh shit." and laughing. She guides me over to the seats and sits me down. "Well that's more like it, vomiting on your ex, a fantastic first impression."

All my senses are exploding I can't think or speak, I knew something had been going on since she changed jobs, but I wasn't ready for this. Every sense in my body screams at me to get a drink, several drinks, and numb this agonising pain. I can still feel this girl's hand on my back, reassuringly smoothing from side to side. I need to replace the alcohol I just lost from my system, I can't cope with consciousness right now I need to blur my vision and blind my mind. The purple girl keeps whispering to me but I can't make out what's being said. Eventually able to speak I manage "I think I need a drink, I don't want to remember this."

Chapter 1

The Christmas market is bustling with life, thousands of visitors coming to indulge in their festive spirits, most hand in hand with loved one's. Whereas I'm sat with my phone in one hand and my head in the other, rubbing at my temples trying to alleviate the pulsating pain of this migraine, I clearly had one too many last night. Fortunately for me, no matter how busy the market gets, this stall very rarely has customers. In a Market full of tantalising foods and cheap trinkets there doesn't seem much of a demand for expensive handcrafted chess boards all boasting such eccentric design and colour. Plenty of people stop to look at them, admiring the craftsmanship and making plans to buy one "later" which usually translates to never. They'll loudly boast "I'm gonna get that one. Obviously not today but probably next week." And I never see them again, unless it's to boast to someone else their infinitely prolonged plans. As a result of this I have a lot of free time at work that I try to spend wisely. There's a small collection of books under the counter, collected by me and my uncle to combat boredom. When we bring in a book and finish it we leave it for the other in case it piques their interest. I also have an assortment of pens and a lined pad with which I try to write a piece of poetry everyday, just to give myself a sense of purpose. Sometimes I find it helps me understand how I actually feel without a fog of ignorance clouding my mind. Most of the time I hate what I write, but when I finally created something I liked, I sent it into the letter column of a local paper. I just assumed they wouldn't publish a poem in a section usually reserved to complain about buses or road works in the city. But to my surprise my little piece about why people seem so alone in such a busy city was printed right there for the city to see.

The following days even saw some readers writing in, commenting on my poem and discussing the topic. Since then I try to write at least 1 good piece a week, something I feel is worth submitting. Sometimes they don't even print the ones I submit, that always stings. My head is still feeling waterlogged from whatever I drank last night, and so writing something feels like a far more challenging task than I'm used to.

Worst of all, in my fogged state I'm struggling to decide on my title. I guess I can use both.

Stream to sea or time and the flame

By Patrick Terret

I remember when I was young

And

Everything was bright and brilliant

And

Time worked as we were told it would.

Then when things became difficult life continued

    on that advance.

    Forever forward.

Then things became different, suddenly I was free.

I did not know that freedom is a dangerous toxin.

Then when things became difficult

Everything stopped.

    Time sped up.

    Life slowed down.

Ugh it's appalling, but the best I'll be able to produce today I imagine. I guess it could be worse, I'll just have to settle for mediocracy today. At least I was able to reclaim my mind from Nat for a short while, which is a victory in of itself.

Five minutes later and I'm on Facebook. I'm not looking at her profile. That would be a pathetic mistake. I'm just scrolling through my feed, not looking for anything in particular. Until I find what I wasn't looking for and stop dead. A post by her. A change to her cover picture, a nice looking picture of everyone from last night, except me of course. Oh wow she sure is leaning into Jason. I type "Bitch" into the comments and don't post it. It's not passive aggressive if I don't actually post it, or maybe that makes it worse.

Fifteen minute into rock bottom I find a picture with me in it. It was posted by a Heidi William's that I assume works with Nat. I don't have any recollection of the selfie being taken, but I'm stood close behind her wearing a weary smile and tired eyes. Maybe the picture is a cruel display, she was in on the joke perhaps. Or maybe she felt sorry for me and didn't want me to feel so left out. I study the picture again and notice a girl in the background staring at us with a level of intensity. I feel as if I recognize her face from somewhere yet I can't place it. The lights of the club cover her face and hair in a purple glow making it more difficult to recall.

I'm suddenly snapped out of my deep concentration by a familiar voice, "Well, well, well". My gaze darts up from my phone to meet the inquisitive eyes of Nigel Fuller. I feel them reading me. "You look like shit." he continues, gesturing at my hunched body balancing on the stool. "Was it that bad?" he asks, making a third attempt to initiate conversation, I nod in response. "See I told you it would be. Is this rigor mortis setting in?" He asks, again gesturing at my odd position. I smirk, a genuine appreciation for his presence lightening my mood. "I wish, death would be so kind-"

"Oh shut up." He interrupts, leaning over the counter as best as he can "So your death was purely emotional? Is that why you're being so emo?" He laughs lightly and I can't help but join. "So are you going to say some kind words at the funeral?" I ask

"For your emotions?"

"Obviously."

"How about, Patrick was always a dickhead, and now since this dreadful loss, has become an emo dickhead."

I chuckle "I think it needs more emphasis on the dickhead part but otherwise perfect."

Nigel steps back grinning, proud of improving my mood I'm sure. Despite our bashful type of friendship we care for each other deeply. He keeps the conversation going for me, "So who was that on the phone?"

"I wasn't on the phone I was just looking at pictures."

"On your phone idiot, but I didn't mean now anyway, I was talking about last night obviously."

I stand inside the hut, perked back to life by intrigue and company. "What are you talking about? What happened last night?"

Nigel leans back and claps loudly "Holy crap maybe you were as bad as she said! How much of last night do you remember?"

I don't remember much at all of last night. I remember looking down from the balcony, spying out Nat below. I remember throwing up and nothing else. "Let's say nothing, what do you know?"

Smiling wide he throws up his hands "Ok ok ok let me start, so I was getting a beautiful early night of sleep. That is until I get a call about 1am, then a second which I answer, eyes still closed. And what a surprise it's my best friend Patrick, slurring down the phone making no sense. Then I hear him arguing with a girl demanding his phone and suddenly a stranger is telling me you're ok and she's putting you into a taxi and do I know your address."

I blush, ashamed at my lack of sense and amnesia. "I don't know who that was, did you give her my address??" I ask concerned.

"Well I gave her your apartment building, not your floor or room."

"Thankfully I still made it back in. Thank you man I'm sorry I woke you."

"Don't worry dumbass, that's why I came to visit you in wonderland, I was worried about you. Kinda didn't expect you to be in work though."

"Everyday is hell, so a hangover doesn't make much impact."

"See an emo dickhead, my eulogy was spot on." He let's out a wild laugh over his joke and I join in, tickled by it.

"Maybe it was the girl in this picture, Heidi something." I go to show him but he's already started talking.

"Probably, when you were arguing about your phone it sounds like you dropped it."

I examine the dent freshly chipped into the top left of my phone. "So that's what that is."

"Yeah then when you were in the taxi-" Nigel continues, but I cut him off, unable to stomach anymore embarrassment. "Stop that's ok that's enough now. What's the point of drinking to forget if you just remind me?" I joke, a joke he appreciates as he bites his tongue and then let's out a sly chuckle before speaking again. "So since my evidently correct advice was ignored last night, and you suffered for it, does that mean you'll see sense tonight?"

"The house party?" Nigel has been trying to get me to go his friends party for close to a month now, I've always been evasive with my answer.

"Most certainly." He grins.

Well I guess it is an excuse to drink in a judgement free zone, and Nigel will be able to look after me. "Ok I'll put my faith in your judgement. Just this once."

"Awesome!" He beams from the other side of the chess boards, and turns to a middle aged woman that had appeared next to him, inspecting the boards. "Really good stuff, I'd recommend wood above metal." She looks at him like he just shit himself and walks off. He turns back to me and shrugs "Old bitch. Anyway enjoy however many hours you've got left, but be out by 6 so I can meet you at the bus stop by mine for half past."

I give him a nod again.

"Half past." He repeats, retreating into the crowds.

I move the seat closer to the heater and rest back down on it, holding my hands on the heater to warm my fingers. The massive open window is bringing the cold indoors.

The prophesied party

Damien came back to close up early, giving me a head start to get home and prepare myself both mentally and physically for tonight's party. The pleasant surprise gives me more time to hopelessly cry in the shower, what a win. It also allows me to get back to an old hobby of mine as it's been a while since I've been low enough to consider shower drinking a viable solution to my problems. But low and behold either the tears or whisky worked as I'm feeling relatively better now. The situation still sits dormant at the back of my mind, a looming threat waiting in the shadows.

20 minutes to go.

I put on black Jeans and button up my Burberry shirt. The shirt was a gift from my uncle, which once tight on me, now hangs a little loose as I've not been eating regularly the past few weeks. I add an extra touch of mess to my mousey brown hair and apply the contents of an aftershave tester given to me by Nigel.

10 minutes to go.

With physical prep done it's time for mental prep. I finish the pool at the bottom of the bottle I had been cradling in the shower. I suck on the pacifier as my opium of choice burns down through my throat extinguishing the flames of anxiety and pain I harbour, quenching my desperation.

5 minutes late

I found a few more drinks scattered about the apartment, and so now with my vision blurred I'm ready to head out and meet Nigel. The journey ends up taking me 20 minutes on account of distractedly dancing the wrong way a few times, and stopping to breathe on a bus stop for 15 minutes.

25 minutes late.

When I finally see him waiting for me he's smoking on a bench. Tut tut.

He looks up to see me approaching and calls out "Yo dude what took you so long? You live like 5 minutes away."

"I got lost." I say, feeling very little guilt.

"It's the same 4 streets you walk every day, don't tell me you've started already?"

My face blooms red "Of course not." I lie.

He scans my face so I back up the lie "I just needed some time with the emotions you know?"

I can read him as well as he thinks he can read me so I take relief in seeing his face soften and shoulders loosen. He believed it.

"So essentially you were just crying like a bitch?" He kindly asks.

"Essentially yeah." I confess.

"Hey, just know anytime you need to talk to me I'll be there to listen bro, I know you'd have my back if I ever needed it. And I promise I wont mock you until at least the day after." He awkwardly laughs, clearly unwanted I lay this conversation to rest by saying "Thanks, good to have you. How far of a walk is this party again?"

"Oh not far like just up that way." He says traipsing in the general direction.

30 minutes later.

"I just thought it was in the neighbourhood is all, that's what you led me to believe." I complain as we finally reach the road.

"Well yeah it's not far out, we should have got the bus." he scolds accordingly.

"Well yeah why didn't we?"

"I forgot to suggest it, here now anyway so what's the point in what ifs?" he stumbles on up to the front door, clearly I'm not the only one indulging in a few pre drinks. With a single knock the door is opened by a short man in a red velvet suit with. The host of this party, though I don't remember his name. He looks to be dressed for a dinner party. The host beams at Nigel who says "Well hello there my guy." To which the host replies in a voice like satin, "Well there you are, the whole party has been waiting to get started in there." With this he let's out a controlled chuckle and they begin shouting at each other about various topics, Nigel slurring and laughing whilst the host maintains his overly soft tone despite it's volume. After a minute we are led inside, the host puts his arm around me, leading me in whilst smoking from a pipe.

The inside of the house is already full of people bustling and shouting in conversation with one another. Most in groups some as pairs, little conversation camps set up all down the hall. Nigel keeps loudly greeting people down the hall way, treating each greeting with the excitement of friends long parted finally reunited, and yet I'm sure he sees most of these people a few times a week. Someone calls out "Pat." And I just nod in the general direction of the crowd.

We finally make it through to the living room which fittingly is full of life, and a far more crowded environment than the hall had been. I crush myself against the wall as Nigel does his rounds of introductions. From all angles I'm bombarded by party goers loudly slurring drunk conversation, some incapable of stringing a whole sentence. What's worse is they're all so uninteresting, conversations based around work and weather, staying skin deep only considering the world. Conversation should be about the self, the world, and the universe. Firstly the self as most every action effects us on a personal emotional level or our internal emotional choices guide us to act and effect the world around us. The world is work, weather, friends and anything else that exists in our reality. The universe is the unlimited realm of possibilities that could occur outside of our understanding, dreams, fate, a higher power. Everyone here has restricted themselves to 1 dimension of conversation. Safe conversation.

I'm feeling claustrophobic so I push my way through the ocean of mindless chattering and head towards the door. I'd rather exclude myself from these successful socialites, all likely capable of initiating empty conversations with strangers. Just because I'm incapable of communicating am I less than these people? As I reach the door to the hall I look back to see if Nigel has noticed, but luckily he's too busy indulging in his social connections to notice that I'm not fun. I weave around the formations in the hall, heading towards the kitchen when I get a light scent of the perfume I bought for Nat last February as a birthday present. I spent far too much time trying to find the perfect representation of the feelings she pioneered in my heart. I did too well though because that smell of is nothing but Nat now and I can see her in my peripheral everywhere. A chasing phantom talking in every group. Sounds smells and sights all become Nat and I desperately hurry my way to the kitchen. Immediately on my right is the fridge which I open to look purposeful. The cool chill from inside starts to numb the burning pain in my head and I move my face deeper into it's glow. For a second things feel as if they might be ok, but then an icy shiver rushes down my spine and the muscles in my back contract.

I stand away from the fridge and close the door, I wrestle my coat off in an attempt to cool the burning across my body. Thankfully the kitchen is far less dense than the living room or hall so I make space on the kitchen counter and put my weight against it. As I stand leaning on it I close my eyes and try to focus on the world. I only see one world. A world lost. I see the glimmer of a smile on her face as she unwraps the perfume, her concern asking if it was as expensive as she thinks. I see her eyes deepen, unblinking, as I explain the process and reasons behind my choice. The first I love you. My heart weeps as my brain seeps all the best moments painting a landscape of perfect times. An unconscious selection of memories that deceive me into thinking things were all good and could work if things went back to how they used to be. I try to focus on her new job, on the lies, the mistakes. My heart rate is pounding to loud in my ears to hear the rabble of the kitchen and I feel the kitchen counter sway under my weight as if on a boat at sea.

I'm at the zoo. The weather is perfect, sunny and complimentary to the outdoor environment. Natalie is excitedly leading me around, she has been all day. She insists on seeing every animal and I insist on not leaving her side. Ever. She talks to every animal in a mothering way and names them all. She's talking to Sid in a mock lazy voice as he hangs from his branch. "They're so lazy, they're so lucky how do I get to sleep all day?" she asks me. I know it isn't real. I know I'm changing bits, it was raining, and the animal act began to feel tedious and annoying. But my mind is in a better place than my body so I allow myself this indulgence. "The best way to sleep all day is in my arms." she giggles

"I wouldn't want to sleep through time with you, I'll save dreaming for when I'm without you, as you're all I want to see. My dreams are real when I'm with you." She moves to hug me whilst saying this but I suddenly feel her holding me from behind. I can feel it. I'm not imagining it.

"Patrick are you ok man?" I know the voice and reality drops back in. I open my eyes and the illusion is shattered. I ended up sitting at a stool sprawled over the kitchen counter as if asleep, as if in a dream. I turn to look at Nigel, who has his hand on my back and is wearing a face of concern. I give him a puzzled and tired nod. "Was it another panic attack? We can leave if you need." Before I have time to answer him the host bursts into the kitchen with the energy and presence of a full orchestra. Above his head he's holding aloft 2 boxes of beer cans, "Marianne misplaced the party bags, I certainly hope these will do!" . He drops down the cans on the counter with a thud that quickly mutes the room for a second. "Sorry guys!" The host leans towards me "I wouldn't open them for a while if I were you." He whispers, raising his eyebrows and pulling an incredibly over dramatic face, maintaining eye contact with me.

"Thank you" I sheepishly reply, unsure what to make of the character still trapping me in his gaze. "So Nigel says you make chess?" he enquires, leaning against the counter and retrieving a beer.

"Well I sell chess sets that my uncle makes." I say

He pauses before taking a sip "Oh that's awesome, I've never played chess is it any good?"

"Uh yeah. If you have the patience for it I guess." Unsure of how to continue a conversation about chess with someone who's never played it, I quickly redirect the conversation to take the social stress of talking off myself. "So how did you meet Nigel?"

He grins at the opportunity to take the stage. "My life was blessed by the inferno of Nigel years ago, the poor fool was in the same drama course as me, obviously he wanted learn everything he could from me, isn't that right?" he asks, pointing his can at Nigel and spilling some. "No no no man it was that pub quiz! No the game night that was it."

"Ol yeah that was it! You remember that bird?" Suddenly the host's tone makes a drastic change, the gentrification he exuded had vanished.

"Which one? The blonde one with..."

"NO man the ginger one with that sour face on her."

"ANYWAY." Nigel interjects "You're trying to avoid that I won that tournament."

"THROUGH BUTTON MASHING NOT SKILL."

"You what? You almost broke their controller smashing random buttons so hard."

I'm only half aware of this chat as my mind pieces bits of old information together. Yes Nigel introduced me to Nat. She always did look sour I guess, on account of her small lips I think. Even Nigel's reaction leads me to believe. I'm sure I'm just looking for it to be true, like there's a great sense of fate in the universe and everything will work out ok.

"Oh man I would have smashed that girl though." My attention is suddenly reclaimed by the host, possible misunderstanding and yet my chest is already tight.

"Which one?" Nigel asks for me.

"The one that done that house party with all the football stuff on the walls and she had a kid."

"She had a kid??"

"Yeah she was like 27 or something."

"Fuck she looks good mind."

Feeling safe I phase back into my mind, occasionally nodding and laughing if it seems appropriate. Most of their stories are about girls anyway and that's the last thing I want to talk about. But yet again I'm dragged out of my thoughts, this time by Nigel tapping my chest and saying "Yeah this guy got boggled out of his mind last night as well. Couldn't even talk on the phone."

The host returns to his calm softer tone I had first heard, "Well that's always the sign of what was clearly a great night, what on earth was running through your veins?" He leans closer to me again, eyes reading me with depth.

"Uh- just a few drinks." I confess.

He pauses and let's out a hearty laugh "Atta boy!" He then changes focus again "You know Alan right? I got so drunk with him the other week at Rocco's thing."

I stop paying attention now and start scanning the other guests in the room. I recognise a few faces in the crowd but no one I'm that well acquainted with. Friends of friends and that guy I know does water reviews on some online blog. My eyes turn to the strangers, a girl in white and black chequered dungarees with soft dark skin, circle glasses, and wild curly. I skim across a few more girls and suddenly stop at a girl with her back to me. My eyes drawn to the vibrancy of her silk purple hair, matched by the equally eye catching bright green sweater she's wearing that's at least 2 sizes too big. As I watch she flaps the excess sleeves about as if trying to convey something, or perhaps an odd dance. My eyes linger hoping for a slight turn to glimpse her face. When it comes I see just how beautiful her features are, she's deep in laughter so I'm treated to deep dimples and the cutest smile I've seen. Her teeth are near perfect with the front 2 being a little big and crooked which adds a great deal of character to her happiness. A smile starts to form from the warmth of what ifs. She notices my glazed stare or half smile because her eyes suddenly dart to me and she stops laughing.

Oh shit.

I look away quickly to avoid any negative outcome.

"PATRICK?!"

I look back quickly in confusion at her bounding towards me through the crowds, Nigel and the host stop their conversation abruptly as she pushes between them to get to me.

"Now I can't believe you aren't following me." she jokes, gracing me with the sunniest of smiles.

Beauty without boundary

Free from my head I'm sprung into the world, unprepared and unsure as to the true nature of these events. For the first time in quite a while I'm more interested in what's happening before me than what's happened before to me. All my anxieties hushed in preparation for what the real world might be about to offer me. Eyes wide and alert I stumble on the words "Oh hi, hey, how are you?"

She laughs and jokingly taps my shoulder "What about you? Are you ok now? Not even hungover?" She eyes the can in my hand "Oh did you not even stop? Yeah the best way to cure a hangover is to drink it off." With these Words, a small portion of the puzzle's answer is resolved and my sub conscious starts piecing a solution together.

"Wait you know Patrick?" Nigel chimes in.

"Obviously, Patrick's great, who wouldn't want to know Patrick." she continues joking, moving closer towards me as she does.

"But since when?" Nigel continues.

"Since last night, he made a mess and needed a saviour, I'm always happy to help." By the end of this, fragments of last night rise to the surface of my conscious mind and I begin to remember her. She's also reached her destination as she's now leaning next to me on the kitchen counter.

"Oh fuck! Was that you on the phone? Totally didn't recognize your voice isn't that odd?" Says Nigel, and I almost sense an essence of spite in his tone.

"Yeah well it's been a few years and phones are soulless machines." Replies the purple girl.

I speak up, as this is my situation "To be honest much of last night was lost in the alcoholic amnesia so I didn't recognize you at first sorry."

"Oh I thought that's why you were smiling at me."

The host makes his voice heard again "I think it would appear that Pete simply liked what he saw, and as a man of honesty I must say who wouldn't?"

"Oh? You liked what you saw did you Pete-rick?" She sticks her tongue through her teeth and winks at me.

I have a choice to make, a crucial choice, as to whether I want to be forward or play it safe. It's to my discretion to decide if she's being flirty or friendly. I'm drunk enough to make the bold move. "Yeah I had quite a nice view." As slimy as it sounds it works as I receive a "Yes man." from the host and the girl laughs and moves even closer into me, sliding her hand behind my back.

"Ha yeah who wouldn't." Jokes Nigel, finishing his drink and retrieving another. "So what exactly happened to Patrick last night?"

"Oh he threw up everywhere and so I had to sit with him for an hour, during which we had a lovely loud argument with the ex. Then after those fireworks he needed help with the stairs and had no way home, so I had to carry him and speak to the taxi people. Then he tried calling you, after which we spent 10 minutes trying to work out his address for when the taxi arrived."

I can feel myself flushing red. I can't remember any of that, was I really that bad? Or is it a joke?

"Jesus dude." Nigel responds, with an odd tone I think is concern.

"Live every day like it's your last." I successfully pull out of my ass to the fanfare of the host who calls out "Yeah he's got it!" and angles his can in toast to me. The girl grabs my forearm, "I'm going outside for a smoke, are you coming?" Feeling without choice I nod and follow. Behind me I hear the faint voice of Nigel "But you don't smoke".

The bitter cold of the night mocks me for not bringing my coat out with me, sending shiver after shiver down my spine. As I shake, I watch her select a cigarette, as if unique in a way only she can see. I'm offered one as she continues to inspect her selection. Pausing with her lighter, she outstretches her hand to me, offering to light mine first, after which she stands watching me, her cigarette still unlit. "So I wasn't all that memorable last night then?" She asks with inquisitive eyes.

"Don't take it personally." I reply "Very few things are."

She cocks her head and lights her cigarette "Somebody's cocky. What about Nah-tali-ah?" She teases.

I don't tense up. I don't feel any burst of pain. Instead I find myself laughing at her mocking pronunciation. "Who?" I joke.

"That's a good sign." she smiles lightly punching my shoulder, which in the cold sets off a reaction through my whole body. "Woo sorry don't know my own strength." She giggles.

"Didn't think to grab my coat from the side and that just unfroze my nervous system." I explain through the chatter of my teeth.

"Oh what are you nervous about sweet? I don't bite." It's refreshing for everything to lead into a joke as opposed to the icy cold serious nature of Natalie. "Are you not cold?" I ask, eyeing the lack of anything covering her legs.

"Nope." She declares "I've got my big coat covering my chest, all warmth comes from your core so if you keep that warm all of you can be warm. You just have to have mastery of your body and mind." She gleams a big proud smile. She doesn't get a response as I stand vibrating, choosing to discard the remains of the cigarette to free up my hand to work on warming myself. In one long drag she says goodbye to the remainder of her cigarette and tosses the last quarter. "Well I am warm even if you don't believe me, let me prove it." Her arms wrap around me as I'm locked in a deep embrace. I sheepishly hug back, and sure enough I can feel a great heat emanating from her. Apart from the external warmth I feel from her hug, I feel a warmth spread from my chest as a world of opportunities open up. Time stops and allows me to appreciate every detail of the moment, cradling the radiator. She smells of lavender and expensive perfume and smoke, surprisingly the perfect combination. The moment is shattered by the sudden intrusion of the host's voice, shouting out the open kitchen window behind us, "Hell yeah! He got in there then! Nice one lad." He and Nigel are sat on the counter leaning out the window, Nigel using the frame for support. "Silver tongue does it again then Pat. Happy for you man." He retreats back inside, seemingly put off by the cold. The host, still leaning out, imparts a last piece of advice, once again adopting vapid posh tone "Might I recommend not wasting this chance Pete, there is a gorgeous girl waiting to be kissed, and if you don't do it I'm happy to oblige."

I look at her.

She looks at me.

We fulfil the audience request.

For as amazing and life fulfilling of a moment it was, it didn't impact. My mind went blank during our contact. Maybe it impacted too much and my mind couldn't process it so it left it blank. The only way to find out is to attempt the experiment a few more times.

Oh when I felt it I sure felt it. A million light pulses flashing in my mind, an array of magical colours illuminating such indescribable emotions. Of all drugs, her lips hold the most allure. So impactful is this moment that the cheers and whistles pouring out the window are silenced. During a pause for breath she pulls out and holds aloft her phone "Oh yeah did you want this?" she asks.

"No I already have one thanks."

"I meant my number dummy." My eyes slowly focus in on her blurry screen. Perhaps I'm just blurry.

"Oh. I was joking, playing the fool is all." Pulling out my phone I see a missed call. Nat. I go to my contacts and copy type in her number 1 digit at a time, repeatedly checking I'm not mistaken. "So what do I save you as?" I enquire, keen to finally discover her name.

"You can call me Bunny."

"Why?"

"Because that's my name?" She looks at me like I'm stupid, desperate to escape this humiliation I don't question it, instead simply typing "Bunny" with a heart into my phone.

We moved indoors because I couldn't stop bitching about the cold. Music was pouring from the front room and so she led me there, a homing pigeon searching for a vibe. All seating was pushed as far against the wall as possible to create a fairly successful space to allow people to dance, although not many had taken this opportunity. Unsurprisingly all seating was occupied as it had been when I first arrived. Bunny lets go of my hand to head towards the closest seat, crouches and starts talking to the guy there. Having nothing to offer whatever their conversation, I hold back by the door, surveying the room for my own potential conversation. At that moment I notice the guy she is talking to stand, his face a shock of rage, and storms towards me. I tense and move back as he moves straight past me and storms down the hallway to the kitchen. I look back at his seat, now occupied by her, offering a proud smile to me and patting her lap. "How did you do that?" I call over the music, perching myself on the arm of the sofa. "I know people, like his girlfriend, and his girlfriend's work mate's." Her face suddenly drops "Oh shit sorry, not a good example."

"Why?" I ask

She shakes the cautious look off of her face "Doesn't matter. Why aren't you on my lap? That looks uncomfortable."

Nervously I laugh, "I can't sit on your lap." I begin.

"Why on earth not, you don't seem heavy and my thighs are awfully strong." To reinforce this point she gives them a firm slap.

Still unable to stop my laughter I protest "I can't I'm a guy."

"OH that's bullshit! You were fine with me looking after you last night!" she taps the girl sat next to her on the shoulder. A girl with her head shaved aside from a single dreadlock of toxic green hair "Eve! My friend, Patrick here has had a very rough few days and he's feeling exhausted, is it alright for him to lie out?" Eve's matching green lips spread into a genuine smile as she nods at me and says "Sure." To Bunny. With an offer too good to refuse she doesn't wait for my answer, instead pulling me down onto her. I make myself comfortable led across them with the arm of the sofa now serving as a head rest, holding my head up high enough to talk to Bunny. "Thanks I think I needed some rest, I've been going pretty overboard and not sleeping." I shout over the invasive music.

"Yeah I could tell dude, you were swaying a lot. And you told me the same thing last night." She moves her head down onto mine, pressing our foreheads together and closing her eyes. I do the same and allow the vibrations of the surprisingly good sound system to vibrate through my bones. The vibration is most apparent through the contact of our heads. Perhaps mentally linking and making a connection on a far deeper level than physical. Alternatively, I'm still very drunk.

My concentration remains on Bunny for several hours as the party landscape changes around us, with no effect on me. My gaze is firmly placed. The alcohol seemed to lose it's effect on me as I became intoxicated by a more potent air between us. During our fixation on each other the party had undergone a change in atmosphere from a fairly reserved gathering to a high energy crucible for mistakes. The first event which sparked this shift was a fight that broke out in the kitchen, no one had attempted to stop the guys, instead spurring them on. This first display of anti social acceptance served as a sign to everyone that there were no rules in this host's land.

The front room is now crowded with people taking full advantage of the space cleared to dance. The use of drugs has become far more relaxed as no one seems to feel the need to hide them. The host has impressively created a lawless society at this party in just over a few hours, the masks worn by the people were lifted allowing their true desires to guide their actions rather than social etiquette. Truly free.

Bunny has been dragging me from conversation to conversation, doing her best to involve me in everything that doesn't involve me. A kind act, perhaps an unconscious one, but as I'm fairly nervous and not good at communicating I feel overly touched by this. She seems to be friends with a lot of guys. Not a problem. Probably. I mean Nat was friends with Jason. No I can't think like that stop she's been out of your head all evening, don't let her ghost spoil a good thing.

Eventually the whole party has congregated in the front room to dance to the odd mix of songs being chosen by everyone. Amongst this sweaty mass of people, me and Bunny do our best to dance with each other, I'm hindered by a lack of space and a lack of coordination. Still, she keeps laughing sincerely so I think it's working. I swing my arms like they're twice their length and sway my body. Nigel refers to my style of movement as feather dancing, as I dance like a feather uncontrollably thrust by the wind. I think I look more like a puppet, only moving certain points I'm confident controlling. Bunny isn't dancing much better, she does a lot of finger guns and head shaking. A hand grabs my shoulder and I spin to face Nigel, a line of blue glitter painted across his cheek. I point at it and loudly ask "Who did that to you?"

He grins "War paint!" He calls back, clearly unable to hear me over the impressive sound system.

"Not what I asked." I begin but he cuts me off by shouting back "They're crazy! The shit I've done tonight! What have you got?" He points to Bunny, whose hands I feel join around my waist from behind.

"A kiss and a dance." I shout back. He pulls a stupid face and shakes his head. The host emerges from the crowd behind him, a wild grin across his face. His well groomed hair now a mess, his red velvet suit lost, replaced by a long fur coat and orange trousers. His face is also decorated by glitter, but far less reserved than Nigel's. "Alright sunshine? Heard you've been pulling at my party?" He gives a knowing nod to Bunny behind me "Well done good sir!" He gives me a heavy jab in the chest before pointing to a bruise on his neck and disappearing back into the dancing crowd.

I spin back to Bunny, pulling her in close and biting away.

The night continues.

The night ends.

"So" Shouts Nigel, perched atop a stone wall, as if a lecturer about to address an audience "How did you, Lord Charming, manage to score with Bunny?" He half heartedly chuckles, lifting his bottle to swig.

"My apologies, but I can't help being irresistible to ten's, hope I didn't show you up too much" I playfully taunt back.

"Pfft! A ten? Bunny's an 8 at best."

"Still makes her twice as hot as you."

He clutches his chest and contorts his face to horror "Agh! My most trusted friend chooses to stab me in the heart, to betray me, by claiming I'm a 4." The bottle in his hand drops and smashes before me, which I swiftly step back from to avoid the spray of shards. "Without me as your wingman you would never have pulled that 8, like the great Caesar I've been killed by those I loved most." He launches off the wall, clearing the glass shards on the ground and landing safely next to me. He then acts out being stabbed and dying for far longer than needed, I still laughed throughout though.

"I doubt your ego is at all fragile so I'm not listening." He laughs at this and abruptly stops.

"Seriously though man, go careful, Bunny has a reputation, and I don't think she's good for you."

"Oh bullshit, I don't fear a man-eater." I chuckle.

"It's not just her, I know how obsessive you get, I have delivered unto you a new form of obsession to serve as distraction." He bows gracefully "You're welcome."

"I won't become obsessed." I protest

"Caught lying again young man! She will consume you. trust me, I know you dude."

Coffee break

Nigel really does know me far too well. As soon as Damien left me to my own devices in the hut I began my hunt for her social media, a task I expected to be quite easy given her bombastic nature. I couldn't have been more wrong as I sit here 2 hours later with nothing to show for my time. I went through all the respondents to the party on Facebook, nothing. Looked through Nigel's friends, also nothing. Same story with Instagram and twitter, so she's not in contact with Nigel I guess. Quite a few customers have come and browsed our stock, a few tried to catch my eye but they wouldn't have bought anything, so I continued searching. I do give in and indulge a few fleeting customers who enquire the price and vanish.

Back to my search. I check all the social accounts for the club we met at, Blue cliff, and no Bunny to be found. Reaching the end of my tether I concede and let Nigel win with a text

"Hey man, how's the hangover?"

Three long minutes pass.

"So anyway what's Bunny's Instagram?"

For 20 minutes I sit with my eyes transfixed on my blank phone screen, waiting for the notification light to brighten my mood. A customer appears at the window and begins speaking to me, an older gentleman in a black tidy long coat with fine white hair swept back, and a strong bushy moustache. "These are certainly remarkable, you can see the craftsmanship just from looking, you can tell just how much passion goes into every piece"

"Yeah, my Uncle spends the year carving all of these as a hobby, so come Christmas he has a impressive amount of good quality sets to sell."

"I see so they're family made and sold, that's rare these days. Adds quite a value to them I'd say" he ponders admiring a piece held just before his squinted eyes.

"I have 2 of these sets in my own apartment, made as gifts by him. Family is important to him. And they're of a great quality"

"I can certainly feel the weight of these pieces, and how much is this set here?" The elderly man holds between his fingers a king piece, sculpted to resemble the head of a deer, eyes hollow. A strong smile holds across his face.

"That one is 70, but we do have a cheaper alternative that still has those particular pieces for 50" I motion to a slightly smaller variant of the same set behind me on the shelf.

"Not necessary, this is a beautiful piece and I'm more than happy paying 70 for the soul captured in this work." He finishes inspecting the king, coated in a blood red paint, and returns it to the board, directly in front of an opposing pawn. The pawns are sculpted to resemble horrified, sometimes screaming human faces atop a pyramid. The deer stares down it's pray standing directly before it. I present a small wooden box and open it to reveal the red velvet interior, into which I place the pieces from the board one by one. The old man reaches inside his coat and presents a bundle of notes wrapped in an elastic band. "There should be about 100, if not slightly more, keep the change for yourself. It's rare to meet someone of your age so well spoken and polite. You're an interesting young man"

In a state of confusion and shock I unfold the bundle and start counting the notes. "Thank you for such an incredibly kind gesture, but I'm sorry there's 120 here I can't accept this"

He let's out a hearty chuckle, deepening the smile lines across his tanned skin. "Yes you can I won't hear otherwise. Merry Christmas" And with that he collects up the board, balancing the box on top and strides off.

I look again at the cluster of notes I'm still gripping, and separate 70 to go in the box and fold the other 50 into my coat pocket. As I lock the money box back up I notice the light on my phone flashing, sure enough a response from Nigel sits waiting for me. Disappointingly it only says

"LOL. Told you."

Due to his irritating response I read it and don't reply. He may well know me too well, but I also know him too well. Sure enough being ignored works and I see the notification light flash again.

"I don't think she uses any kind of social media, kinda hippy I guess."

Mysterious enough to hold my intrigue, I won't be able to clear my mind until I understand

"How did you meet her then?"

I'm treated to a fairly quick reply.

"She was on the same acting course as me, we performed Romeo and Juliet together."

Well that seems odd. One thing I recall from the first night I met Bunny was her calling me old. I've been drunk both times we've met, yet I don't think I'm mistaken in recalling she's claimed to be 18 more than once. But Nigel did that course a while ago in college. It was an 18+ course, so Bunny would have been too young to be on the course. Or she hasn't aged? In reality, she must have just lied about her age, but why?

I dig for more.

"What was she like?"

"Excuse me"

I look up to find a customer peering in, eyes bouncing back and forth between products. She has jet black hair tied up in a ponytail with bright azure hair clips contrasting. She appears to be late 20's and is quite beautiful. "How can I help?" I ask, more enthusiastic than intended.

"I'm looking for something specific, do you have the set with the deer heads and the pyramids?"

How odd to have a second customer so soon and for that customer to be after the exact same ugly product.

"I'm sorry, someone actually bought that one about 10 minutes ago" Her expression changes as her deep eyes dart to mine, like a deer in headlights she takes a second to process. As I go to speak again she walks off without a word, retrieving her phone seemingly to make a call. What a weird woman. I didn't even really get chance to talk to her before she ran off. Taking some time to reflect on what just happened, I notice a song that played last night echo through the market. At the centre of the market is a festive bar, constructed mainly of wood, it's a beautiful sight. Boasting 2 levels containing a bar, plenty of seating and tables, and a large Christmas tree in the centre. It can be easily found by the music played on the sound system from open to close . I think the bar staff get choice of songs. There's a little radio in my shack that's still yet to be used on assumption it'll be drowned out. I let the song guide me through memories of last night.

I'm broken out of my daze by the realisation that my notification light is violently flashing, my phone calls for my attention. I scoop it up and check to see 4 missed calls, 1 from Nigel but no message to answer my question. My gut lurches as I also see 2 from Nat, this sensation ceases when I see the final call was from Bunny. Instead, my body is robbed of all feeling as I sit frozen for a sec. She contacted me first. I don't believe it. Not even a text, a call. And so without hesitation I call back.

It rings out 5 times, each feeling like a lifetime. My stomach a mess of nerves.

She answers.

"Hello! Who's this?" She asks.

I clam up, fear dripping off me in the form of sweat. Had she forgotten last night when she awoke, called me earlier out of curiosity for the new mystery number sitting on her phone. "It's Patrick" I cautiously reply.

"Like the starfish? I don't know any others"

"No, we met at a party last night" I uselessly babble.

I can hear her laughing down the other end and heart pauses in apprehension of what she'll say next.

"Being forgotten sure does hurt doesn't it buster?" She laughs again.

All the tension falls out of my shoulders and I feel a level of ease wash over me in realisation of her trick. "Don't worry I wont forget about you again" I play into her hands.

"You'd better not" She proudly retorts. "The cute boy in the cute hut had better not forget me"

I bite the inside of my cheek and smile "Neither of those are as cute as you think"

"I disagree. I think both would look a lot cuter with those Christmas lights turned on though"

I look to the Christmas lights pinned to the inside wall of the hut, almost always absent of life.

Then my attention quickly shifts to the crowds bustling past the hut. "How did you know about them?"

"You look so cute when you're confused" I hear this before the phone can relay it, serving as an echo. I hurriedly stand and lean out of the hut to the best of my abilities. She hangs up. Leaning against the side of the hut Bunny stands with a glowing smile. She gives me a reserved wave and moves to the opening. As I'm lost for words, she fills in the silence. "Wow this place is nifty huh? Oh no way these are the chess sets your Uncle makes?" She picks up a Christmas tree shaped bishop from a red and green Christmas set. "They're better than I thought they would be. No offence! Didn't think they would be bad, but they're shockingly good"

"Thank you, I'll let him know beauty sees itself in his work." I cringe and bite the inside of my cheek. Thankfully she laughs and I don't sense any spite.

"That's poetic I like it" She stops fiddling with the green tree and picks up the opposing teams reindeer.

"Thank you. I do write poetry, I haven't got good at it yet though."

Wide eyed and excited she asks "Can you write me something?"

"I can certainly try, no quality can be guaranteed though." I don't usually write about people, more ideas and events, although I guess her arrival in my life was quite the event.

She does a few literal jumps up and down "That's amazing! I can't wait. When do you finish work?"

"I think my Uncle will be back in a few hours around 4"

"That works perfectly, I have some Christmas shopping to do. See you soon Patrick" She winks and walks, looking back at me a few times laughing.

I pick up my phone to another missed call, and text my Uncle saying:

"Can you get back for 4 today? I have a date"

Excitement passed but still shaky, I take my seat again, taking from a board a rabbit shaped piece.

My incredible amazing Uncle arrives back at half 3, in high spirits. "Hey hey Romeo, it didn't burn down then?" This same question is asked every time he comes back, I don't even know how I could set fire to it. "Still in one piece" I reply like every time. He laughs, also standard. "Was it busy?" He asks, unwrapping his long scarf and knowing the answer.

"I got a tip from a sale today"

"Wow, that's never happened, how much did they give you?"

"£50, do you want half?" I ask, already outstretching a hand with 25 in it.

"Don't be ridiculous, you earned that not me, use it for your date" He insists, waving away the offer.

"I just got lucky, it's your hut. Come on you do so much for me."

"I don't need or want it. But I do need and want you to have a good time. I raised you too well. How was that party last night?" He changes topic to end the debate of manners.

"Surprisingly the best party I've been to"

He pauses taking his coat off, face stuck with shock "Really? So you're doing better with parties now?"

"No I just got really lucky, hence this date"

"From the party?" A warm smile spreads across his face "My man showing me how it's done. You definitely deserve that tip"

"I was quiet and reserved like always, she did all the work"

He throws his coat past me onto a spare stool. "Well then sounds like you've found a keeper, I got you something for your date" He unfastens his messenger bag and pulls out a small glass bottle that he throws to me. Thankfully, I catch it.

"I don't need any after shave, you've already given me plenty."

"Good because that's perfume, I didn't realise when I bought it. Give it to her or something, it was £60" He takes his place on his stool, cushioned by his coat.

"At least let me buy it off you for 25 then" I argue

"Shut up and go meet your date, do me proud"

I text Bunny and tell her I'm ready whenever she is.

She let's me know she'll be here in 5 minutes.

Not keen on my Uncle embarrassing me, I leave the hut and go wait at a seat across the way from it, far from my uncles influence. A few minutes later she bounces up, full of life and energy.

"Look what I found! A fallen angel" She takes a seat next to me as I go to stand, abruptly dropping back down awkwardly.

"Did you find what you were looking for?" I ask.

"Yeah I think I did" She replies, holding my gaze.

Being the weaker man I look away quickly, in doing so I notice my uncle watching intently from the hut. He notices my head turn and raises a thumb up, grinning.

"So where do you want to go?" I ask, already moving to stand.

"Coffee? I think there's a place here that does authentic Italian coffee"

"I'd rather get away from work" I complain. "There's a place I usually go that's just around the corner, does the best coffee"

"Awesome! Let's go put that to the test"

Local coffee shops just have an atmosphere about them, they calm and comfort me. This one stands leagues above the rest. The walls are lined with book shelves collecting together the finest pieces of literature. The air is intoxicated with the warm rich smell of freshly ground coffee beans. The staff seem to really love being here as much as I do, always happy to give as much as they can for customers. For example the girl taking our orders enthusiastically took Bunny through all of the different tea options, something I wouldn't have the patience for. The sunny girl serving eventually recommended a tea that Bunny agreed to and I bought the drinks. They make them up for us in cute take away cups, with a picture of a coffee bean in the centre of the sun just above a line saying "Best roast you can buy" Bunny reads out. "Mine doesn't even have anything roasted"

"Yeah you suggested coffee, why didn't you get coffee?" This small quirk almost annoyed me, I don't understand why as it's so insignificant. We bustle out from the warmth of the coffee shop into the biting chill of December wind. The sun is beginning it's retreat out of sight, creating a beautiful feeling in the dimly lit dusk, illuminated by just a few rays of golden sunlight between the buildings. Bunny keeps her mouth perched on the lid of her tea, a portable heater.

"It's getting dark" I begin, only for Bunny to jump in and cut me off. "You're right, let's go somewhere fun"

I guess retreat isn't an option and I have to push on trying to impress her with my awkward demeanour. "Any suggestions?" I ask.

"I know a place" she grins.

The place in question is somewhere I've never heard of before, yet seems to fit Bunny perfectly. It's a bowling alley, as well as a bar, arcade, cinema, market, and dancing venue all in one establishment. All the different parts are pretty connected and visible in an open space, offering a unique environment for sure. I'm not sure if this place feels too pretentious for me or if I'm just annoyed that I didn't already know about this multicultural mesh of entertainment options. Even still it's pretty, I can't deny that contrary to my spite. From the ceiling hang vines of warm coloured fairy lights flickering like stars beneath the artificial sky. The arcade and bowling lanes are illuminated under coloured lamps, washing the lanes in a vibrant blue, and the arcade section in contrasting green and pink. This gives each it's own sense of life, individuality depicted through colour. Bunny bounds back from the front desk "We're on lane 8" She calls as she directs me towards the blue mist. I'm unquestionably awful at bowling so this choice of date isn't ideal for me, especially considering my nervous attitude around this girl. I take a seat as she sets up the scoreboard, attempting to type purple princess but running out of characters, so instead settling for Bunny. I'm treated to the name "Pete" which I fail to understand at first. She senses my confusion and deletes both names, instead typing out Venus and Mars and selecting start. I watch her with great intensity as she selects a ball, aims and rolls. I cheer with despair as she hits a strike, sending my hopes of keeping up clattering down like the pins.

"Your turn Mars, show a lady what you can do" She flirts taking her seat next to me. I take my time selecting the right bowling ball, attempting to prolong the inevitable. "Nice balls!" Bunny jokes and claps for herself. It doesn't matter what happened next let's just forget it. I didn't get any points though. Returning to my seat in shame Bunny calls "Valiant effort though!" whilst clapping and reassuringly laughing at me.

"I'm going to go and grab some drinks, maybe it'll help me play better" I announce.

"Ooooh excellent idea! Let's find out if drunk Patrick is a better bowler than sober Patrick"

"So what would you like to drink?"

Her order memorized I head up towards the bar to buy them. However the bar is more popular than I realised as I'm greeted with a human wall in my way. Through great effort I'm able to push my way through a couple of layers to the bar itself. For 5 minutes I'm shoved and pushed about by the crowd waiting to be noticed, but finally I'm able to catch the barman's attention and the drinks are ordered. I pay more than I should and turn to make my way back towards Bunny at our lane. I freeze dead in my tracks. Before me stands the last person I wanted or expected to see. Her hair a frizzy mess and make up hardly done, Nat stands there wearing my expression of shock and discomfort.

"Patrick" she mouths, seemingly unable to find the power to speak in this moment. Confronted by her mistake, on display at her lowest. Whereas I've been relatively well off since she betrayed me, fate has favoured me by pushing me into the path of Bunny twice until we hit it off. I say nothing, continuing my scowl. She also remains silent, looking away from me every few seconds, and then looking back pained, as if looking away might cause me to disappear. In her mind it may seem like a bad dream perhaps. We keep being pushed by drunk patrons trying to get to the bar, or simply exist in their limited space. I'm not ready for this, I can feel so many unchecked emotions swirling up during this silent encounter, and so I turn and push my way through and out of the congregation of drunks. As I escape the crowd and make it to the small set of steps down to the rest of the venue I hear Nat shout my name. I pause on the first step down, turning to look at her. She's already started crying and I can feel my heart bleed in response. We both stay frozen again, this time free of the crowd, afraid to make the first move and praying for the other to act first. She goes first "I'm sorry, can we talk? I want things to work."

This gentrified girl

This request hits me with such immense force I feel all my faculties shut down for a second as to avoid over working and blowing my mind. In all my intrusive wild day dreams I had never foreseen the possibility that Natalie would want to work things out with me. This had been beyond my realm of hope and dreams. It seems too good to be true, in my pain I hadn't even thought about what it was I wanted, about how to get her back. In fact I find it odd, I was focusing on the pain and wanting the past back, but the idea of working things back out hadn't really occurred, maybe I didn't want this. She had, after all, betrayed me and so it seems right I have the moral high ground and don't need to subject myself to her mistreatment again.

"I'm sorry if you need time I understand if you do, but can we at least start talking about this please?" She tries to reason with me, still stood dumbfounded, eyes wide attempting to read every detail of this new world I've just entered. My eyes read her for a second, hair frizzy and unwashed clamped on top of her head, make up minimal making her look a little ill, dressed in comfy messy clothes rather than dressed up. "I don't think there's much to talk about, I saw what I needed to."

She scrunches her eyes and lowers her head in response to this, face leaking a red tone. "We need to work out what happened between us, to find out what the hell went wrong. Something as important as what we had shouldn't just be left to die on account of dumb decisions." She finally builds back the courage to face me and lays shaky eyes upon me, eager for any sign of love in my response. It takes self control to not immediately cave into the future I held by my heart for years. The woman stood before me is a totem of my loves and dreams. With her I discovered a lot about myself and the world, and every inch of her is a reminder of that, an unshakable nostalgia for home. My eyes break from hers and drift over her shoulder to the bowling lanes, where Bunny sits bathed in blue. Even at this distance I can see the dimples setting shadows as she smiles down at her phone. The purple hair glows like a beacon in the ocean. My eyes return to Nat, her frizzy orange hair spilling out uncontrollably, the harsh light of the bar making her face look gaunt, almost unrecognisable. A single tear trails from her eye, painting a black path down her face, to great effect as she says "Please don't give up on what we have."

"What we had." I correct her, feeling clarity and confidence in my choice, for once I am choosing my destiny. She stands speechless, processing the blow to her heart as I walk past her and return to Bunny.

"Hey I took your go, you're welcome. You actually have points now." She giggles when I arrive "Oh check out this video too isn't it adorable?" She holds her phone aloft so I can see the video playing on screen, an all white rabbit is nibbling the corner of a shopping bag to get at what looks to be carrots inside. It is quite cute and Bunny seems to be enthralled by it, so I let it soften my heart. "He's adorable, trouble maker though" I appraise, handing her drink.

"She" I'm corrected.

"How do you know?" I ask.

"It's my rabbit." She takes a sip of her vodka and coke, sliding through pictures of the rabbit on her phone. "What's her name?" I take a seat next to her.

"Snow white" She smirks, taking another sip.

"I'm sorry I took so long, do you think we can go somewhere quieter after this? I want to hear everything you have to say"

Her cheeks go purple in the blue light "Yeah of course" She replies, a tone of shock present.

I put my drink down and take my go, glancing over at a dance floor adjacent to the arcade, Nat is with a whole group of her friends, she isn't dancing, resting her head on a girls shoulder. I can't see if she's crying. I have no idea if she's seen Bunny with me. I fail at my go again and Bunny reassures me whilst laughing at my failure. I keep a cautious eye on the dancefloor for a few minutes but soon forget why and embrace my time being humbled by Bunny. Lightly elated by the drinks we sit laughing for a bit after the game has concluded. Silence soon becomes the topic when we find ourselves locked into one another's eyes. After a few minutes interlocking lips we make an effort to leave. By the door way I see Nat sitting next to a guy on an old rustic Victorian bench, talking and looking distraught. We don't make eye contact but I notice her sights on me as I pass. I stop walking, turning away from her and grabbing Bunny, pulling her in we kiss passionately for a few seconds and we walk out the door without looking back.

"Well you didn't do that bad!" Bunny's attempt to console my poor performance falls on deaf ears as I contemplate my true victory. "That was good I'm glad we went."

"Oh you ended up enjoying bowling?"

"What? Oh yeah, even though I did terribly."

"You managed to score 12 points, that's 12 more than you had at the start of the game."

"You scored 8 points on my go"

"You still got 4 then" She laughs and hugs me.

"Where can we go from here?"

"Oh you didn't have any suggestions? Luckily I'm here to save the day again." She boasts "Follow me." She needlessly requests, already dragging me behind her.

We travel through the still busy streets of night, bustling with Christmas shoppers feeling the countdown coming to a close. Maybe I should think about getting Bunny a present for Christmas now, and soon as there's only a week to go. Bunny stops us every few often to recount her stories of the places we pass, and in some cases just to admire grand displays of Christmas lights. I don't mind, the addition of vibrant colourful lights only accentuates her beauty.

"Where are we actually going?" I finally ask, reaching a tolerance for sight seeing.

"Rich part of town!" She proudly declares.

"So what, a cafe or bar?"

"Or a bench, or a curb, I'll have all the beauty I'll need. The grand architecture of the lavishly rich and that gorgeous face of yours."

She's crazy. I don't think I've met anyone as enthusiastic about existence as her, everything is a marvel to her eyes, it's wonderful in a sense. "Ok let's go find a rich curb to claim." I concede.

It becomes clear when we enter the wealthy territory from the buildings doubling in size and age, with Christmas decor so extravagant it puts the Christmas market to shame. The monstrous stone houses all around illuminated by their extravagant selection of reindeer and snowmen, complimented by nativity scenes and enough dancing lights to outshine the sun. Bunny hops to take a seat on the wall of a 4 story house built with evident passion of beautiful sandstone. The garden is lavishly decorated with Greek pillars of stone and a dry marble fountain, all suffocated by strings of crystal white lights. She and I kiss for a few minutes on this wall until we're disrupted by the shout of a disgruntled resident calling from his window. The sudden noise causes Bunny to jolt from the wall, seemingly landing clumsily on the curb, only to majestically spin on one foot back towards the house and proudly raise two fingers at the inhabitant. It was a well performed display of agility. I'm almost shocked she was able to react so quick. I join in the taunt and Bunny begins walking off, I aptly follow.

Seemingly with no destination in mind she carelessly dances through the quiet streets, regularly looking back at me and smiling, motioning for me to dance with her. As she dances her colours transition through the colour wheel of Christmas decor. Her face is continually redefined by her ever moving relation to the lavish lights. Her dancing begins to change as she swings her arms around a little more carelessly and the look on her face becomes almost sly. She's mimicking my dancing from the party, but in a far more elegant style on a far grander stage. I check the windows of the houses around and find no one watching, all occupied with the worlds inside, I look back to Bunny and see her smile. Feeling safe I begin to join in, self consciously moving my arms as if they were weightless, taking every movement slow so I can think it through. Bunny jigs up to me, "That's more like it, there's the dancing queen I wanted to see" She chuckles, moving her feet, torso, and arms in a sophisticated variation of my dancing. I let go. I begin to freely dance with her, laughing and singing as we wander through the night.

After half an hour of this trip through heaven we wearily find a bench to rest on. The bench is in a small oval park surrounded by road and houses. A thick assortment of trees and bushes provide cover from the surroundings though, as if a secluded island in the middle of an urban sea. We lean into each other on the bench, attempting to catch our breath.

"Your stupid dance is pretty fun when you lose yourself in it" She pants.

"It's like a reaction so I don't have to think" I reply during breaths. I'm using the breathing techniques my uncle taught me when I first started having panic attacks, so my breathing is calm but I'm still exhausted.

"I guess it is just mindlessly flailing your arms about, it's damn beautiful though" She exclaims, sitting back.

"I've been told it looks like a duck trying to put out a fire"

"I meant the town, the streets, the lights, this park"

"Oh" I mentally retract a second. "I hate this place, I feel trapped in a concrete maze"

"What? This place is awesome, all the beautiful lights and exquisite architecture?"

"I mean this whole city, I've been here for so many years and watched it change and decay, morph into an abomination of home and hell."

She looks at me a little startled, good job idiot you've scared her off already.

"Well..." She takes a second to look in my eyes "When are we going to escape?"

I look at her puzzled, surprised by any outcome other than worst case scenario. "Escape?"

"Yeah escape this city, do we have anywhere to go? Maybe get a boat and live in the ocean? Definitely no concrete mazes out there." She grins.

"Ocean works, or maybe somewhere with more than 5 trees?" I motion at the lone sentinels in the park.

"It's settled then, once we acquire a boat or a forest we will escape this city by night."

I sit, captive to her energy and unpredictable nature, as she suddenly regains her energy and bolts up from the bench. "But for now, will you survive in this city with me? And search for the beauty in this mundane place."

I join her standing. "I will."

She unleashes the widest smile yet and heads towards the gate, waving a pointed finger at 4 floor house across the road. "Look how big it is and how extra the door is, calm down you're not that tall mate. Your doors don't fit."

This makes me laugh. Bunny has a wonderful ability to switch from too well spoken to drunken slur in an instant. It keeps all conversations with her interesting. This sudden change in dialect seems like a lowering of her guard though which is a good sign.

"You don't know the original owner, he might have been 8ft for all you know. Or he was compensating heavily."

"Look at the incredible display of colours though! It's surreal like a dream."

"And next month the wonder will be gone and the world grey and colourless. I can only bare this place during Christmas."

"Then we'll find our own colour. And then the world! Tokyo maybe?"

"I think I can do that" I smile.

"You're shivering again? Are you cold? Or do you always just tremor in my presence?" She playfully asks.

"Now we've stopped dancing I'm starting to feel the cold"

"Do you think we can do a roly poly down that hill? Although that's a good excuse to dance and I'd rather do that. Let's go!" She glides backwards out the park gate, waving her arms up in front of her effortlessly. Her chaotic energy wins me over and I join.

Within 10 minutes the rain had started, catching us both unprepared. We dashed down the streets, coats overhead, searching for cover. There's a square a few minutes away with a large covered section I'm leading us towards. As we approach it I can see a great many other people also taking refuge under it. Mingling amongst the crowd I notice everyone is looking the same way, at a building across the street. A big screen on the side of the building appears to be showing a film. Bill Murray is on screen wearing a suit and looking annoyed, I haven't seen this one. Bunny wraps her arms around me and squeezes tight. "Provide me warmth or I will die." She jokes, squeezing tighter. With nowhere to redirect attention I ask what's on my mind. "So how old are you?"

"Why?" A sharp change in tone.

"Well I remember you calling me old more than once, but Nigel seems to think you were in his class?"

Her arms detach from me and she steps back. "What else did Nigel say about me?"

"Nothing, he was too busy boasting about the drugs still in his system."

She breathes deeply, "Yeah I was in his class, I was just saying you looked old, I wasn't saying you were old."

It feels like a lie but I let her continue.

"But yeah I was in drama class with him, a few years ago. Basically the same age."

"So you're 21?" I ask.

"I was. Until September."

"You're older than me?"

"Barely! When even is your birthday?"

"Late July"

"Ok so like a year between us that's all"

I stand in confusion, what was the point of such an unimportant lie. A water drop rolls down her face, I'm unsure if it's on account of the rain or a tear. "Wow. You're so old" I joke, putting my hand on her shoulder. She looks up lip trembling, eyes watering. "Don't make fun of me she." She squeaks. I pull her back into a hug.

At the end of her street I finish hugging her and kiss her head. "So when are you next free?" I ask.

"Tonight wasn't free! You owe me 100 by the way" She laughs. "What are you doing tomorrow?"

"I don't have work, so currently nothing."

"Well then you're meeting me at noon." She winks and begins walking off.

"Where?" I call out, "I don't know what noon is."

I get no reply.

On Stranger tides

My phone wakes me the next morning, vibrating furiously on my bedside table. I miss the call as it drags me out of the nightmare leaving me disoriented and confused. Upon the second chorus of vibrations I stretch out and grab it.

"Hello?" I wearily ask.

"Hey honey! Did I wake you?" The chirpy tone revitalises me like a hit of strong coffee.

"From an awful dream so don't worry I'm grateful."

"I'm your saviour once again then! I'm going to start charging for this ya know?"

"I thought you already were?"

"Oh yeah! Time to rise my rates I guess. You're going to need to give me a lot more affection to pay it off."

"I think I can manage." I roll back into a comfortable position on my bed. "Do you always wake up this early?"

"Patrick it's almost noon"

"What the hell does that mean?"

"You're a poet and 21 years old, how do you not know when noon is?"

I pull my phone away from my ear to check the time, 11:35. "Oh, that makes sense, sorry I lost track of time whilst asleep."

"It happens to the best of us, are you going to leave this damsel distressed without you?"

"I don't even know where you want to meet?"

"That coffee place? It seems like the mid point between us."

I agree and we make a few minute of small talk before Bunny tells me to hurry and I comply.

I get to the Coffee shop a little after noon. She's sat at a table, legs crossed wearing a super oversized green jumper and large thin glasses with gold rims. She sees me and waves me over cheerily. I saunter over and fall into the armchair opposite her. "It's 12:52." She comments, taking a sip of her hot chocolate and fogging her glasses. "I missed noon slightly" I admit, unzipping my heavy coat.

"If you weren't so cute I'd be mad." She teases, eyes reappearing through her fogged glasses.

"Well then I'm glad you can't see or I'd be in trouble."

She takes another sip of her drink, freshly fogging her glasses again. "What do you mean?" She asks.

"I'm going to grab a drink, any ideas what to do after?"

"A picnic?" She suggests, pointing to the black clouds lingering in the sky outside.

I order a mocha and put my change in the tip jar. The girl that serves me draws a smiley face on my cup and writes "The one and only" before my name. I thank her again and return to my seat.

Bunny is sat chewing her glasses looking at me thoughtfully, in her hand is a copy of Fahrenheit 451, held open by her thumb. "Are you enjoying that?" I ask.

"The book or my glasses?"

"Either?"

"Neither are as exhilarating as your company." She assures me.

"It's an old book, I've read it, how far in are you?" I ask.

"I've already read it, I just enjoy revisiting the classics sometimes. I like how in the end they manage to keep something so important alive through memory."

"Do you read a lot?" I begin warming myself with my coffee.

"Not really, I guess I kinda do but not in a weird way."

"How can you read in a weird way?"

She switches topic, "So I was trying to think of what we could do, are your parents home?"

I put down my drink and shake my head.

"Really? A free house? How awfully convenient and warm. When will they be back?"

"Not for a while." I reply weakly.

"Problem solved!" She cheers. "I'm going to get a mince pie to celebrate" She declares, already making her way up to the counter. I pick up the glasses she left on the table and try them on, no magnification in the lenses. I fold them back onto the table.

An onslaught of questions are fired at me on the walk to my apartment block, I avoid answering most. Her energy is off the chart today, she's wildly over excited. In the elevator she exclaims how lucky I am to be able to ride a horizontal train every day. Her weirdness is certainly a part of her charm. With my key in the door I pause and warn her, "Cleaning rarely happens in my place, so it's a little messy."

Bunny walks into my world.

"Wow look at the furniture!" She gestures at my old armchair, "That's too groovy to be so casually placed in your living room." She continues sleuthing around my apartment, loudly complimenting the things she likes, and laughing at things she doesn't. "I didn't even realise these things were real." She claims, admiring my grandfather clock in the corner. She rushes to the window, "The view! You're on top of the world!"

"I feel like it." I say, hugging her from behind.

She leans back into me for a second of quiet before springing back to life "Which room is yours?" She excitedly asks, heading to the bathroom door.

"There's only one bedroom, that's not it."

"Wait you live alone? That's so cool! How do you afford this working in a silly hut?"

"My Uncle pays for it, the same man who's hut you just called silly."

She looks at me impressed, "Sorry Unk." She says carelessly smirking before opening the door to my room "Why does he pay for an expensive apartment for his nephew?" She inquires, searching for the light switch.

"Because my parents are dead."

She stops looking for the switch and turns back to me, reading my face for the punchline. "well that's not funny." She finally says. Well done Patrick, delivered with the subtlety of an elephant on a elevator. "Yeah you're telling me." I finally reply. "It's ok though, I've been lucky to have my Uncle to look after me. He seems a little rough around the edges and immature but he's done very well for himself, and do whatever it takes to make sure I'm ok."

Closing the door behind her, Bunny walks over to me, still a puzzled expression on her face as her eyes scan mine for a last sign of a punchline. She finally settles on her belief and her face shapes to pain. "I'm sorry." She says, before embracing me in a hug, squeezing tighter than ever before. I hear her sniffing, as she buries her face deeper into me. "That's so fucked up, I'm so sorry." I hear her say, muffled heavily by my jumper.

"It's ok honestly, are you crying?"

"Yes!" She pulls away to display her red and tear streamed face, "How could I not be? That's so sad and you're so nice."

I'm now forced to comfort her over my misfortune, seeming a little unfair, I hold her for a bit, stroking her back and kissing her forehead, then sit her down and head off to make her a cup of tea. She continues taking a tour of curious glances around my room, from my green coated chess set to the grandfather clock and beyond. I bring her a mug of tea and sit across from the grand armchair in a camping seat Nigel uses when he's hear. The only other person to visit me is my Uncle who has too much energy to sit. Oh and I guess Nat used to use it, but we mainly used the bed to rest. She slipped my mind. "So did your uncle make that one too?" She enquires, pointing to the chess set beneath my TV.

"Yeah he's made me quite a few, that was the first one he gave me, it was my 7th birthday. Green was my favourite colour as a kid"

"It looks so nice. Could you play when you were 7?"

"No, but he soon taught me."

She glances back to it, "Think you could teach me?" She cautiously asks.

"I can certainly try."

Bunny continue sipping her tea whilst I retrieve the set and make space for it on the table. "Which side do you want to play?" I ask her, dragging the table more central between us. "Oh definitely green!" She pauses visibly, "Actually no, that was your favourite colour, I'll let you play them, I'll be on the wood team."

"It's ok, my favourite person can play my favourite colour." I spin the board 180, presenting her with the green army. "It's not even my favourite colour anymore"

"What's your favourite now?"

"Purple"

I raise a pawn "These can only travel forward and can only move one space, except on their first move at which point they can move two. They capture sideways though."

"Sorry can you repeat that? I was too busy blushing."

I smirk with appreciation that my flirtation paid off, and lower the piece with decreased desire to explain.

"I'll just put on a YouTube video to explain."

Bunny watches the colourful demonstration play out on screen, holding aloft each piece as they become relevant. I envision the cogs in her head absorbing and storing information. I'll still likely need to explain things as I go along, but at least she has a base understanding of it. "Ok got it let's play" She cheerfully decrees.

Being resigned to the white team I go first, moving the pawn in font of my Queen forward 2 spaces, Bunny counters this move by copying it. I then move the pawn standing ahead of the King forward by one space, a move Bunny also copies. When playing chess I usually play black, allowing for a reactionary play style where I can devise counters rather than lead the way, and so this play of mimicry is throwing me off. But then Bunny knows no strategy yet, I'm taking it easy on her for this reason. She stops mirroring my moves by reacting to the movement of my knight by moving her bishop. She's biting her lip and taking a damn good look at the battlefield. I feel a movement in my heart, a sort of elation I can't place. Perhaps excitement or pride, anticipation of the unexpected?

Outside the window, from the deep skies falls the first flake of December magic. A singular snow flake dances from the heavens to earth, falling unnoticed amongst busy crowds, melting on impact, a unique snowflake forever unknown. Although this one had very little impact, the billion more on their way certainly will.

To my surprise Bunny has me on the defensive, having taken 5 of my pieces while I only possess 3 of hers, I'm shocked to discover the mind of a tactician in her head as she responds to my advances with what seems to be premeditated precision. An odd subversion of my expectations from a girl who builds herself around her spontaneity. In fact I'm now a little worried by the concept of losing to a first time player. I'm forced to sacrifice my knight in defence of my Queen, but in retaliation am able to take her castle. After this impressive display I choose to speak up, "You're too good at this to be a beginner, are you sure you haven't played before? Are you just swindling me and in truth you're a world class chess player?"

"Well I tried a few times when I was a lot younger but I guess I was too young to pick it up, am I doing well? And we haven't made any wager for me to swindle from you."

"My uncle has been teaching me since I was a kid, and I appear to be losing so yeah you are doing well. We can put up a wager for the winner if you'd like to add more excitement?" I have a few ideas in mind when suggesting this, yet I'm again surprised by Bunny, queen of the unexpected as she replies, "Ok, if you win we can go into that bedroom for a few hours and you can show me if all your moves are as good as your chess moves. And if I win we do the exact same thing."

This leaves me incapable of replying, I've never been a wildly sexual person, and if she's as insatiable as her personality suggests then I don't even know if I'll be able to satisfy. After a comment like that silence is the worst response,

I'm aware I need to say something, but that comment caught me so off guard that I'm unable to form any words. Instead turning a deep shade of maroon. I hear her giggle as my brain screams at me to say something. She beats me to the chase though, "Awww I'm sorry are you flustered? That's for the purple comment earlier. Relax though man I was talking about yoga." We maintain eye contact for a few seconds as she battles to keep a straight face, eventually losing and releasing her smile and more laughter.

"Deal." I agree, feeling the heat in my face.

The game ended, the winner claimed their prize, very little yoga was performed. Outside the world fills slowly with the soft white blanket of winter, coating everything indiscriminately in a crisp clean coat. Unknown to us, with the curtains drawn and illuminated by candles dotted about the room, the outside world couldn't hold any less importance to me.

sprawled on my floor, her
my chest, a mutual feeling of
e sit baked beneath the
ght of the candles. The music
l playing softly from her
ail traces up and down the
lectrifying the nerves beneath
ive force caused by minimal

o hers and feel her attention
room, to the mess of
is scattered across my sides
uestion as to which specifically
is she breaks the silence with

?"

us." Along with the list she
pectively. "I don't know what
one is though." She points to a
rray of coloured leaves in
ed.

"That's a croton" I explain.

"Never heard of that one. What[...] heads? What's going on there?"

She's referring to collection of [...] spaced out amongst the plants [...]

"They're famous historical figur[es...]"

"Like a museum, oh my god we [...] museum don't we? So is that or[...]"

"Kind of, yes we do, and no. He [...] so you were close. That one is C[...] there is Julius Caesar. Up there [...] Ramses the second."

"Oh I see, king of kings."

There's no way Bunny could ha[ve...] engraved on the base of the bus[t...] often plays dumb yet seems to [...] chess, botany, and history.

"Wanna get coffee?" Bunny ask[s...]

"Sure."

We get dressed and head back to the living room, Bunny first, who stops suddenly and let's out a concerning gasp. "What is it?" I ask, rushing behind her and following her line of sight to the window. The ugly streets and buildings that usually intrude my view are silhouettes in a white mist of rapidly whipping thick snow. "Wow." I exclaim at improved and obscured view. "I take it we're not going out for coffee then?" I ask.

"Why on earth not?!? It's a winter wonderland out there!"

After mild convincing from Bunny we start layering, I give Bunny a blue jumper of mine to provide an extra layer, along with a scarf of mine. Once layered up we head down to the lobby. Through the glass double doors I can see an inch of snow creeping up from the base of the frame.

"It's been going for a while" I say.

"So have we." She runs up to the door and forces it open, ploughing through the snow. She jumps from the lobby out into the snow. Leaving the first imprint in the otherwise blank slate of the pavement. She crunches an imprint into a few other untouched patches. I follow out slowly, adjusting to the harshness of the cold, even with my many layers on I feel it biting through my bones. My first step onto the snow delivers a soft crunch under boot. Bunny is hopping from imprint to imprint so I jump over to join her. She spins to face me, wide white grin and rosy nose. Beneath her knitted hat I see the wire of her earphone protruding providing an excuse for her to dance gracefully through the snow, abandoning the neat footprints for lines traced through grace. The two of us dance through the storm of white petals falling from the clouds. Happy feet write across the ground of our time together, imprint in the snow. A temporary snapshot of happy times. The snowfall picks up and visibility becomes scarce, so much so that I don't notice Bunny stop dancing suddenly. As I move closer I realise that she's stopped, and on her face I see a look of shock and pain plastered across her unusually pale face. Wide eyes starring into the blizzard seeing nothing. "Are you ok?" I shout in concern. Her vision snaps back and gaze turns to me, the shock gone but a morbid fear worn in it's place. I need to sit down." Is all she says before hurriedly making her way back to the door.

I hurry through the snow to catch up which fortunately is easy as she's leaning all of her weight in to the door struggling to breathe. "WHAT'S HAPPENING?" My desperation increasing.

"I'm cool just need to get upstairs." She sputters, launching herself from the door into the lobby, and stumbling towards the lift. I catch up with her at the lift door, on which she's leaning all of her weight and pressing the button frantically. I quickly pull her arm away so when the door opens she won't fall in, and hold her steady.

"Can you just tell me what's going on so I can help?"

"Don't let me fall. Sit me down. If I die play Crying swimmers or something by Gus that's sad. My favourite flowers are red Rose's so just dump a load of them on the tombstone for me." Bunny keeps a comical tone in her voice for this which I can't help but feel is fake to keep me calm, perhaps even to calm herself. She leans her weight on me as we huddle into the lift and I press the 6. By the 6th floor she can't support any of her own weight so I scoop under her legs and carry her to my door. I sit her down against the wall to unlock the door, she watches on with glazed eyes. I go to carry her again but she's attempting to stand. I help her up and guide her to the armchair. "I'll call an ambulance." I start, but Bunny raise her hand. "No, no I'll be fine now, I just sometimes get a bit weak, I was ill as a child, but basically all better now."

"What triggered it? You were more than a bit weak, you couldn't stand."

"I won't die. But if I do, isn't this romantic?" She murmurs in a dream like tone. "Can you leave the lights off please?" She adds. I comply and sit across from her, watching with baited breath for the faintest sign of things getting worse. "Can I help at all? Do you need water?"

She let's out a weak laugh, "No sweet, it'll be ok, it's a cycle, extreme pain, energy loss, recovery. I'm on the 3rd step now." She smiles at me, wide and forced with her eyes closed. She reopens them and her attention heads outside the window. To the usually grey grimy city painted in a fresh coat of white paint. I keep my eyes fixated on her as she inspects the new world outside the window.

I let her recover for a bit, silence comfortably sitting in the air. Content in each other's presence.

"Thank you." She eventually break the silence, turning her attention back to me.

"You helped me at Indigo Cliff."

"Oh yeah I did, we're both pretty great then." She smiles a golden sincere smile for me.

We both look content at one another.

"I love you." One of us says.

"I love you too." Replies the other.

A Dumb smile lights both our faces.

"I should head home and stop bothering you soon."

"There is heavy snow my love. Please don't go." I plead.

"Are you sure?"

"Have you read today's paper?" I ask.

"Of course not."

Today's paper

Rabbit so bright with hope you always burn
Found me, eyes closed unwilling to learn
Can joy of passion fulfil the rosy lens
Emotions without words referred through pens
In spark was born a mighty fire with blaze
With which I play and stoke in winter days
Count on you to keep me warm oh Bunny
We just begin so let's see then honey
How far we can push for infinity
A lifetime spent in your divinity
Now feels no days of waste can be foreseen
Decided days of hope had come and been
Source in my life will seek to gentrify
Complete the mask self chosen to identify

Snow day

"I don't think I would call you a bad friend. A terrible friend is more fitting. Perhaps I'm just too good of a friend so my standards for friends is too high." Nigel babbles on with his guilt trip, a trick he's used enough times for it to lose it's power over me. I'm nodding along, rolling a snowball in preparation for his next outburst.

"Five calls and countless texts, what if I was dying?"

"I'd have a lot more peace."

"Oh hilarious! Let's all kill Nigel with our words because it's fun."

"Look I'm sorry Nigel, I was busy and I didn't see my phone until this morning." Frustration likely present in my tone. But then Nigel's tone changes far more drastically, seemingly filled with actual aggression, a voice I hadn't heard from him in a while. ,"Oh I bet you fucking were!

Oh so busy with your Bunny." He chokes for a second but begins speaking again before I can formulate a response. "Is it malice or are you clueless? You claim to be smarter than me, but not smart enough to see when a cheap whore is using you."

The snowball departs my hand and collides with his face, causing him to stumble back. I had aimed for the shoulder and so guilt is added to the mix of emotions in my stomach. Nigel sputters and slides through the snow a bit, blinded by the assault. "I don't care about your stupid past problems, you do not speak about anyone I'm with like that, understand?"

Nigel recomposes himself, taking a deep breath before saying, "When she destroys you I won't be here. Then you'll learn the benefits of choosing some dumb bitch over me."

I noticed him call a few times last night, and I saw the missed calls, but luckily his messages assured me it was unimportant. Or at least, less important than Bunny. Then this morning whilst walking Bunny home through the frozen city I answered a call from him only to be bombarded by words. Most rude, but still in his traditional comical sense. He told me to meet him at the park we grew up playing in. Saw Bunny to her road, kissed her goodbye, and headed over to humour him. This park is a massive patch of land populated with trees and play parks and ponds. When I first met him at the gates I could tell he was irritable, but it wasn't until we climbed the largest part of the hill in icy conditions, and sat at the bench we first met, that he let out his true feelings. His level of aggression seemingly too great to be concealed beneath the mask any longer.

It started with petty comments and grew into irritable questioning.

And now I sit here alone, watching from the icy dunes as he stumbles and slides his way to the bottom, swearing loud enough for me to hear on each misstep.

I use the silence as a chance to think and reflect on the current situation, scanning the view of the crystal city. Nigel was always pretty unpredictable, it was the best thing about him, but he rarely argued with his friends, least of all me. I can't think of anything I've done to justify this reaction. Perhaps he's jealous now that I stand stable and happy and he still plays the bachelor life. No, he didn't like Natalie but was never like this, not at all. A warm smile crosses my face, letting out an icy cloud of breath. I had found someone that makes life bearable, I had gotten even with Natalie, the heavens had gifted us with a winter wonderland. Things are feeling pretty great. In fact Christmas is only a few days away. I need to get something for Bunny.

My thoughts become interrupted by the sudden appearance of someone sat next to me on the bench, I hadn't noticed them approach being so intertwined in my mind. I look and recognize the man sat next to me, 6ft 4, heavy muscle, wild afro barely contained beneath a stretched red beanie hat. I know he lives in a tent in this park, I've seen him asking people for money a few times. His clothes are old and worn, but are still quite nice, consisting of a suit and tie beneath a heavy trench coat. He doesn't seem at all cold. He's watching out over the city like I was, with the same great interest. I see his eyes move in my direction through his thick rimmed glasses, so I give him a sincere smile and he gives me a wide one back. In the distance, beneath some trees I can see his tent, coated in snow, it looks almost like tipi in shape. Suddenly concerned I speak up, "Is that your tent down there?" I ask.

He turns his head slowly to it, then to me and nods.

"Have you got anywhere warm to go?"

"My tent is warm enough thank you, but I appreciate your concern friend." He smiles once again.

"No I can't let you sleep out in these conditions, it's dangerous. That shelter down by Bean boy brewery is £10 a night." I rustle my hand in my pocket and pull open my wallet, "I have £30 here that's 3 nights, hopefully by then the snow will be gone."

He eyes the money over the top of his glasses before letting out a deep laugh, "That is an incredibly kind offer, but I have quite enough money thank you. This world seems kind to me, people are always offering me things I don't need. I like to give back. What's your name son?"

"Patrick, what's yours?"

"Pleasure to meet you Patrick. Have you ever heard the tale of Narcissus?"

"Yes I have, it's-"

"In Greek myth, Narcissus was a hunter known for his astounding beauty, but the man had disdain for those who loved him, resulting in some ending their life to please him. He reduced a mountain nymph to an echo with his rejection."

"I know."

He stops and looks at me, wide eyes, stern jaw. I quickly shut up and let him continue.

"The Goddess Nemesis eventually took notice of the damage he was causing and chose to punish him. And so after a hunt he was lured by her to a pool to drink, in the reflection of the water he saw himself, the definition of beauty. Of course he wasn't aware it was just his own reflection and so fell deeply in love. Unable to leave the allure of the beauty in the water Narcissus spent his time trying to obtain the love of the reflection, a feat which was impossible. And as the days passed without sleep or food both he and his reflection grew weak. Narcissus tried desperately to help his love, but it was merely a reflection. In time, unable to watch his love die, and burning from the flames of an unrequited love, Narcissus took his own life. Others say he melted from the passion inside of him and became a gold a white flower."

This wasn't how I expected this day to go, but it is actually quite an interesting change. "Yeah it's an interesting story, good values hidden within."

"Yes there are many values in there worth analysing. He and his love both died on account of a shallow surface level attraction. There was nothing beneath the surface at all. Everyone gets hurt when selfish desire and vanity takes over." He peers a knowing eye at me, offering a half smile. "Just my gift to you, a myth to think about in your spare time. Maybe you'll learn something." I fold a £10 note into my palm and offer to shake his hand. He accepts and I feel something heavy in my palm as he shakes. I look down to see the note still folded there, atop it a small circular pocket mirror. I look back up to see him already walking off down the hill disappearing amongst the thick huddle of trees. He spoke as if he knew me, that was odd. And this mirror, combined with his story, it's as if he's offering advice on a life he knows nothing about.

Regardless, the seed was planted, throughout the day the story of Narcissus kept playing through my mind, triggered by seemingly unrelated influences. Whilst waiting for my coffee I dazed into the tale again to fill time. I'm snapped out of it by the quirky barista snapping her fingers towards my vacant face. "Why are you dreaming when dreams are coming true outside the window?"

"Uh sorry, yeah it is quite beautiful in the snow, but I've just been out for a few hours, the magic has worn off."

"That was quick, well we have a policy about sleeping standing up, so if you want to dream take the comfy armchair." She grins at me in an almost challenging way. I don't think she's flirting, just exceptionally friendly and charismatic. "Aha thanks." I say, turning towards the seat in a daze.

"Wait you haven't got your drink yet fella." She chirps, placing it on the counter.

"Oh yeah, thank you. I'm surprised you're open with all of this snow."

"I love this place too much to let the snow stop me, but good luck to it, I live here." She laughs and starts making the next drink.

I take a seat, slumping into the velvet blue armchair, the luxurious cushions softening the weight on my shoulders. Taking a sip of my coffee I check my phone for any contact from Nigel. No texts, 1 missed call but not from him. Someone less important.

I text Bunny, asking if she's free at any point today, and sit back sipping my coffee.

Snow crunches under my boots with each cautious step. The snow reflects the light of the moon, illuminating the wild forest around me. The trees absorb far to much of the light keeping it dim and difficult to see. I can't remember which way I was supposed to be heading. The trees cast eerie shadows across each other and the ground, swaying slowly in the wind. I stop suddenly hearing another sound come from the woods. Footsteps. It's fast and there sounds to be more than 2 legs speeding through the dark towards me. I look down and see the water beneath me, a vile reflection screaming at me.

"Dude you barely touched your drink, hope you like cold coffee."

The unique tone of the barista reels me back into reality from my accidental slumber. Through a daze I scout the cafe, now vacant of business. Outside of the window the sun no longer shines on the snow.

"I don't know how long I was out for, I think I dozed off."

"Coffee is meant to have the opposite effect, although really you didn't touch it. It's ok the boss already said to make you a fresh one and let you get up at your own speed. We're going to be cleaning for the next hour anyway so don't rush yourself." She cocks her head and smiles.

I nod along to the slew of information before thanking her, my eyes wander behind the counter where I see the manager looking on smiling. A lady in her mid 40's with golden hair and a series of different coloured gem stones decorating all manor of jewellery. She Carries with her a warmth that she translates into her business giving this place a homely feel. I recollect on my nightmare, on the forest turned swamp, and the creature in the woods. A fresh drink is brought over to me with compliments and a round of smiles from all of the staff. This place is too good to me. A copy of today's paper has been left folded on the table, but I don't bother looking, aside from my own work I have no care for news. The outside world has no bearing on me, so the news is irrelevant to me. I don't care who's preparing nuclear arms, if it can't help me understand my situation with Nigel, or reminisce on these beautiful moments with Bunny, I have no interest. Instead, my phone serves as the gateway to all of this, so there my favour lies, as I retrieve it from beneath the circular mirror I had left atop. I've missed a reply from Bunny, but fortunately it was just her confirming she's busy tonight. No matter, I can play chess against myself. The novelty of the mirror returns as I find myself staring into my confused reflection for a few minutes. Concerned thick eyebrows creased in contemplation, my eyes hiding great waves of pain and problems I refuse to acknowledge and validate. My gaze is fixated, as if the sight was an unknown horror to me, I'm incapable of redirecting my eyes. Even when I hear the manager call not to let this one go cold, I thank her and take a sip, still painting eye contact with myself, as if 2 animals daring the other to attack first. The screen of my phone suddenly bursts into light, severing my inescapable standoff. Thrown off guard and confused I answer the incoming call without looking at the screen.

"Pat?" The voice is timid, seemingly afraid, and yet completely recognisable. I've stumbled into a trap.

"Natalie? Why are you phoning me?"

"I'm sorry, I-"

"Didn't I say there was nothing left to talk about? If you're attempting to hurt me again it won't work."

"No I'm sorry I just... it hurts I'm weak I wanted to hear you again, I'm falling apart."

"Yeah I'm doing well thanks."

"No stop please! Don't hurt me anymore please I can't... I can't cope with any more."

"Hurt you? You're the thorny rose, so beautiful and alluring but sharp and painful to the touch." My voice must have raised as the staff are all glancing at me whilst going about their tidying.

"I'm sorry, I never meant to hurt you it was all stupidity. There was no malice in what happened I promise it was just an awful mistake."

I lower my tone to avoid the attention of the cafe staff, "I don't believe a single action you've taken hasn't had an element of malice."

"I made so many sacrifices for you Pat, how the hell can you think I'm nothing but malicious?"

"You must be thinking of someone else."

"I put off accepting that job because it scared you."

"Not for long."

"You're impossible Pat."

"I know. It's my speciality."

"Look this really won't work over the phone, are you busy?"

I scout the room of busy bodies trying to tidy around me and weigh up my options hurriedly. I sense a trap. "Ok I'm not busy, what do you suggest?" Next step, spring the trap.

"Meet me at the Dockyard in half an hour?"

"The Dockyard? That's a great place for a murder good choice, it'll take me some time to get there though."

"That's ok I'll wait."

"In this weather? You'll freeze before I get there, this is sounding more like a trap."

"I don't want to hurt you, see you soon." The call ends and I switch my hand from my phone to the mirror again. A distorted smeared reflection of myself scowls at me curiously. I give the face of the mirror a wipe on my jumper and finish my coffee.

The absence of the sun is felt heavily, causing the temperature to plummet. I walk shakily, hands firmly planted in my pockets in an attempt to keep warmth. No other fool would dare venture out in these conditions, leaving this lone fool to own the vacant streets. A fresh layer of evening snow has refilled the melted patches of road, allowing for just one night free from the invasive noise of traffic. There's no grimy details visible, the world consists only of flat plains of crystal snow, as if the world had reset.

As I get closer to the dockyard the perfection is a little more disturbed, a far busier location forcing more to push through the torturous cold to live their lives. I feel somewhat robbed of the world I had found myself in for far too short a time.

Still feeling suspicious I take a short detour allowing me to get a look at most of the area, scanning the scarce crowd for even 1 recognisable face. Even a suspicious glance. No one reveals themselves, and I see Nat sitting alone on a bench near the water. She seems safe from the cold, wrapped in a large white fur coat covering from head to knee, wisps of orange hair flutter from beneath the ice hood, a lone streak of colour in a black and white night. I approach cautiously, still keeping an eye around. She stands to meet me as I approach, breezing over to me and hugging me. I uncomfortably hug her back, wishing my coat was half as thick. We make tracks through the snow, looking for somewhere more sheltered, nothing is really said, even when we speak nothing is said. We eventually find shelter beneath the large arch doorway of a bank, far too extravagant to serve any purpose beyond aesthetic, or so I thought until tonight.

"Look I'm sorry" She begins, and in an instant the atmosphere becomes heavy and uncomfortable. "I was a bitch, unfair and thoughtless. I hurt you and justified it using your past mistakes, but really there's no excuse for lowering myself to your level in response."

Hmmm a pretty proud self serving apology, she couldn't resist taking some jabs at me of course, she expects me to get angry I think that's what she wants.

"Thank you, I appreciate your remorse for hurting me."

She doesn't reply for a few seconds, stunned or unsure. "Do you have anything to say?"

Of course she was waiting for me to apologise, that was her pause. She knows that I know the things I did wrong, why the hell does she want me to apologise again. "Not really."

I Sense her soul die a little with a sigh, maybe she was expecting something else besides an apology. My mind races trying to read hers, she looks hurt, but not like when she wants sympathy, a real concealed pain.

"Well okay." She weakly says, "It's ok you don't need to say anything if you don't feel like it, it won't be sincere."

I race through previous arguments trying to decipher the meaning behind her words. I realise what has to be done.

"Natalie, I'm confused as to why you wanted to see me and what you think I should say now, can you help me understand?"

A Puzzled look I can recognize consumes her face, anger begins to seep in "An apology perhaps for that very spiteful thing you did, mine was stupidity and an accident with my thought about myself, whereas yours was spite and planning and to effect me."

The severity of revenge can't be measured. No I need to stop picking apart everything she says, I don't want this getting any worse and that's all that can come from such scrutiny. "I'm sorry." I simply say. The anger and confusion drain from her face noticeably. "Thank you." The tension is somewhat lifted from the air and conversation begins. Unimportant chatter to establish comfortable conversation. After about 20 minutes of hollow words played for fun with no real interest on either side she says, "I don't know if we loved each other really, I think we were both just fucked up in the same way, and so claiming to love someone with all our own faults was like a justification of our darker sides." I had never seen such depth from her before, but the seed was planted and quickly sprouting. I felt little pockets of my perspective shift as the truth dawned on me. There was truth in what she was saying, but what does that make me. Maybe I'm not what I thought. "Thank you for telling me that, I see what you mean I think, I don't think you're wrong." Some unsure awkward conversation follows as we both try to come to terms. The cold begins biting a far more bitter assault as the wind picks up, throwing snow in all directions. After wasting a few more minutes we decide to part and get into the warmth, separately. We wish each other a happy life in that empty way and as I turn to walk I hear her, "Oh, just one more thing, we may have been the same kind of fucked up, but from what I've heard she's a completely different type of fucked up, so be careful."

She walks off to avoid my glare, vanishing through the snowy curtains.

Eve

I awoke to a frosty reception. I had left my window askew in the night and the intrusive breath of the cold had sighed through my room. A small puddle had formed at the window, likely the melted remains of snow that had snuck it's way in only to discover how short life is in my room. At first I slowly emerged from sleep, gaining awareness and my senses one by one. This was until I regained a sense of temperature and suddenly jolted awake, shooting under my duvet for safety. I took a few seconds to curl, covered completely by it. Once a little heat and bravery return to me, I poke my head out through the top of the duvet, forming a Caterpillar, in this form I was able to crawl my way to the window and cease the barrage of the cold. Still covered I made my way to the thermostat and turned it up far too high. After completing that I hurried back to bed and remained curled up there until it was safe.

Whilst hiding I called Bunny to see how her day looked. This was the moment I realised it was Christmas Eve. And so after a short panic and loudly questioning myself as to a solution I ended up here, in the nightmare that is Christmas eve shopping. I hate crowds and capitalism and a lack of manners, the 3 key ingredients to a Christmas eve shop. I only really need to sort out my uncle and Bunny. A part of me wonders if I should get something for Nigel in case his funny 5 minutes ends soon, but that would require more effort and time in this layer of Dante's inferno. Sadly Bunny's gift giving isn't as limited as mine, perhaps even trying to rival father Christmas himself, her list seems to never end. Being shown countless boring items for people I've never heard of I nod along and repeat "Good idea." To each suggestion thrown my way. The bloated crowds shift like armies of ants collecting and carrying the pieces needed to build their satisfying Christmas. I keep a pained tight smile as countless people shove past behind me swaying me forward and back. Every release onto the slightly reduced hustle of the street felt like a breath of fresh air, to be held and cherished before being submerged in another crowded shop. The whole day has been setting off alarm bells in my head, the stress from those around me finding it's way into me through osmosis in the sweat choked air. I uncomfortably dart my eyes through the muddled faces as Bunny coos over animal shaped pencil toppers. The faces start looking unnatural, I didn't think people had noses like that or eyes so different. Regular features become alien to me as I start to feel more and more out of place. "I need some air." I breathlessly exclaim to Bunny, "I'll see you outside in a second."

"Oh okay, I won't be long now."

I push my way through the crowd, perhaps too forcefully, but none of them had shown restraint on my space. Outside the shop is a small food court with mostly full tables. As a pair stand and make their leave I head to their small table and collapse into the chair.

A call from my Uncle, I answer to silence. I speak into the phone a few times to no response. The people around me begin coughing, 1 after the other. I watch the Mexican wave of abrasive spluttering wash from one side of the court to the other. As it reaches the other side the origin of the epidemic begins choking as he desperately clutches for his drink, unsuccessfully as he lurches forward and collapses onto the table. Screaming begins to erupt from the court and the crowds and I stand from my seat, backing out of the court. I turn to find Bunny struggling out from the shop. I make my way towards her and she looks at me with fear, which quickly shifts to anger. "Are you okay?" I ask frantically.

"This is your fault. You left me alone." She scowls.

"I'm sorry, we need to get out of here."

"No. You do. Get away from me." She shoves me heavily pushing me back into the crowd that sweeps me like the ocean waves away. I struggle against tide unsuccessfully as I see Bunny bend double coughing. Her eyes dart to me full of resentment as she drops to the ground.

"Are you okay?" I hear Bunny ask me, followed by the loud thud of her bag on the table. I open my eyes and nod, "I'm sorry I had to leave there was too much going on I couldn't keep up."

"It's okay, but I missed you." She smiles placing her hand on mine. "Are you getting food?" She inquires, to which I simply shake my head.

After showing me what she had bought, Bunny suggests going to the quieter side of town to finish shopping, a suggestion with which I happily agree.

The quiet side is still fairly busy, but manageable at least. Far less shops and far less high end, it instead plays host to an assortment of vintage stores and family run businesses. We go inside of a jewellers, searching for a gift to satisfy her mother's demanding tastes. Her words not mine. "What's your favourite gem stone?" She asks, pressing her face against the glass inspecting the rows of gem studded necklaces and rings.

"I've never given it much thought I guess." I admit.

"What a waste." She jokes, "I love opal, look at that thing shimmer." She points to a silver necklace with a small white sphere attached to the bottom. As I lean in I see a myriad of colours dance across it and a blue tinge wash over it. " Oh wow so that's opal? That does seem pretty magic."

"It's beautiful!"

Bunny decides on a sapphire studded set of earrings for her mother and she heads to one of the clerks as I head to another.

Back outside my attention is grabbed by an antiques store across the street, a familiar location my Uncle had taken me to a lot when I was a kid. As the door opens the familiar warm must wafts out, greeting me back. A pleasant change from the crisp icy air outside. I kick a few remains of snow from my shoes before entering. Inside hides a collection of forgotten masterpieces from furniture to prehistoric technology to clothing many years out of fashion. I gaze at the lost wonders with awe, moving from display case to display case, eventually stopping at one filled with an assortment of old wrist and pocket watches. Bunny listens with sincere interest as I recall the time me and my uncle disassembled and old pocket watch and rebuilt it piece by piece. "I like that one because you can see all the cogs inside, it gives you an insight into how much work it takes to keep it ticking. Like a person I guess, we take for granted that all these people just exist but there's so much behind every one of them."

"I thought you didn't like people?"

"I like some people." I reply catching her gaze. "I need to find something for my Uncle."

We scout about for a further few minutes until finally I find something that suits my needs. Back outside in the snow we decide to call a break on shopping and go get a coffee instead, a task we had underestimated heavily. The volume of customers had grown in the coffee shops too, leading lines out of doors and absolutely nowhere to sit. We call it a day on shopping and start heading towards our regular place a lot closer to home. Fortunately the location of it had hidden it away from the desperate shoppers of the Eve, with a few empty tables and a relatively short wait. As my turn to approach the counter comes I'm greeted by the familiar face, "Hey sleeping beauty." She says, "The usual?"

"Yeah and a pot of Earl grey as well please. I'll try and stay awake today." I pay and she passes the orders back to the older man behind her, a man seemingly in his 40's but always with a care free air to him, he didn't speak much but always seemed content. I collect my drink, chocolate dusted on top depicting a neatly wrapped present, and a sunny yellow teapot with steam pouring from the spout.

"Oh that's so cool and definitely not fair." Comments Bunny upon seeing the chocolate gift decorating my coffee. "Don't worry." I say, taking a sip and disrupting the formation.

She gasps, "You monster!" She jokes, pouring a long stream of boiling tea into her cup. "What are you going to do for work now Christmas is here?" She asks.

"I hadn't even realised it was here so I've not thought about it, but yeah the Market is closing today. Usually my uncle gives me odd jobs through the year so I never really think about it."

"Oh that's nice of him, is that what he does as well?"

"I don't know what he does really, he's rich, or at least lavish with what he has. He owns a lot of businesses from time to time but it always switches up and he's often busy but doesn't talk about his own life much."

"That's pretty interesting and mysterious, does that mean you're rich?"

"Haha maybe one day, but he's always been clear since I was young that he will always ensure I live comfortably but won't let me be corrupted by money so young. Even if he dies his will says I get his fortune split over 20 years."

"Shitttt you're all sorted then, no wonder you don't have a plan." This comment from Bunny stings a little and I can't tell if it's intentional.

"I do have plans, my writing I guess."

"Where do you plan to go with it?" She asks.

"I don't know."

MERRY CHRISTMAS!

I'm awoken by the energetic message from Bunny at 7am, clearly very excited by the holiday, whilst I on the other hand am still recovering from the bustle of yesterday. I drag myself from bed and begin making a coffee to stimulate my early morning movement. Whilst the kettle is boiling I return the season greetings to Bunny. Upon returning to bed, coffee acquired, I receive a great many excited blurry pics from Bunny of neatly wrapped presents in colourful paper sporting bows and ribbons. I try keeping up with her spirit until she asks about my presents. I put on Gymnopédie No. 1 and lay back on my bed watching the ceiling. But only 20 seconds into it I find myself moving off of my bed to kneel beside it. I'm unconsciously aware of what I'm doing, but it's easier to keep it out of my conscience. Fumbling under the bed I eventually feel the large wooden box and pull it out. It sits with me on the bed, unopened, for a few minutes as I sit staring at it, contemplating Pandora's dilemma.

"I don't really get presents for Christmas." I finally reply to her. "But I found these which is kinda nice." I send her a picture of a dusty polaroid showing a man and woman in their late 20's hanging from one another smiling. The woman is short with beautiful piercing blue eyes, and strong facial bone structure. The man, much taller and with a shaggy mop of black hair. Both wear a carefree sincere smile that sits a little too wide on their faces, neither care, the moment is too important. This is also evident from them both wearing oversized bright Hawaiian shirts.

"Haha you look so funny, who's the girl?" Bunny replies.

"That's my mother." I message back.

"OH! Is that your dad? I thought it was you. That's so sweet, how old were they?"

"I'm not sure, I kinda pushed it out of my mind."

her avoid, Bunny
ar you have
ne."

h, "Thank you, I
ow if what I got
d to getting

atter what

an't go out
by all means!"

o way up my
ore than one
as I can
g in a family
It somewhat
how in an hour?"

2 hours later I gir
anxieties and und
veins. The exterio
presumption of a
season seriously.
colours hang fron
lonely evergreen
drowned in lights
catch release and
heart pauses in ar
to talk to. Thankfu
and wild shock of
lurches out from t
a strong hold. She
times before sayir
here thank you! M
hand and leads m
family pictures ob
plastered against
door from behind

be heard, she beckons me up a narrow set of stairs and guides me into her room. The room is smaller than I had expected, littered with house plants and Polaroids stuck to the walls. My eyes glide across the room to her bed, on the wall beside which hangs a canvas print of Mars and Venus by Botticelli. "Wow I love that painting, I didn't realise you did too."

"Oh yeah he's definitely my favourite artist, and that's my second favourite picture."

"What's your first?" I inquire.

She smiles at me and jumps backwards onto her bed, staring up at the ceiling in awe. I follow the line of her sight up and discover a large poster depicting the birth of Venus hanging right above her bed. It's age was apparent from the tattered corners. "You've created your own Sistine chapel? A good choice." I say in a sense of almost wonder. I lay beside her looking up at it. "Every morning it's the first thing I see when I wake up, the birth of femininity and fertility. It motivates me." I glance at her, the genuine joy and satisfaction present on her face, she notices and turns to kiss me before excitedly announcing "Present time!"

She hops off of the bed and moves across to her table top and pulls a vinyl from it's sleeve before gently lowering it onto the player. With the needle placed she skips to her wardrobe flinging it open to retrieve a large box, wooden and decorated with lavish paint colours. She places it in front of me on the bed and watches excitedly. Atop the box is a large sticky note saying

"Dear Patrick, Merry Christmas, I love you." I let a cautious smile spread across my face as I lift off the lid. Inside sit 5 perfectly wrapped presents I pick out a thin papery one first and begin unwrapping, 2 large tickets poke out.

"It's for a specialised art exhibit at the museum in January! They're bringing all kinds of beautiful and rare paintings in to be displayed for 1 weekend only."

"Oh wow that's amazing, I've heard about that, so can I have one of these?"

"Well of course doofus they're your present, they're both for you, you can take whoever you want." She raise her hand to her chin and poses.

"So you don't want to go?" I ask.

"Obviously! But you don't have to take me."

"I'd love to go with you."

Next I pull out a rectangular flat present, "Is this for me as well?"

"THEY ALL ARE."

"Oh right thank you." I begin unwrapping to find a DVD of the film that had been playing that night in the rain. "Oh I remember this I didn't get to see it very well that night thank you." So she remembers the time we spend together, it isn't just important to me, and the note on the front of the box, does mean the same when it's written down.

"I'm sorry I'm just really sentimental and dumb."

"No, no, I really like it." I assure her, feeling a little overwhelmed. "Should I save these for later?" I ask, still wildly unsure of myself.

"Don't you like them? I'm sorry."

"No I really do but I'm not used to this so it's overwhelming and I don't know if it's rude to open them all at once or not."

A hurt look that had begin to form on her face quickly dissolves and she begins laughing at me "I'm ridiculous, you can open them whenever you want sweetie don't let it stress you."

Her kindness draws a smile wider across my face and releases some of the stress in my back. The next present is pretty nice, a collection of chocolate truffles I had frequently pointed out at the coffee shop. At first I assume the next present is also a DVD, as it boasts the same shape as the other one, but as I pick it up I feel an indent in the front. Inside is a picture Bunny took of us, contained inside a beautiful wooden frame. I run my fingers across the glass pane and thank her quietly.

"You don't have to use it but I think it would look great in your room."

"It definitely will be going there."

The final present is a cube shape and holds surprising weight. I can tell from her eyes this is the one she's most excited for. Inside the wrappings is a black cardboard box, I flip open the lid. It's the pocket watch. My jaw hangs open as I look from it to her to it again.

"How do I respond? I'm really touched but no words can sum up just how much."

"No words at all?" She asks in a hopeful tone.

I form the words in my head and think better of it.

"How about your presents?" I ask, reaching for my bag.

"Sure!"

"I'm sorry they aren't as good but I'm completely lost in all of this, and honestly I forgot that people wrap presents traditionally so I'm it didn't even cross my mind." I grab a scrunch of wrapping paper from off the bed and thrust it into my bag working it around the contents. I pull out an ugly wrapped bell shape, second hand paper loosely hanging off. She laughs and takes it from me "Thank you for recycling, you're saving the planet." She jokes, shaking off the paper which falls away to reveal a glass bell jar with a wooden plinth at the bottom, sitting proudly on it is a wooden chess piece carved into the shape of a rabbit. "That's so cool I love it!" She excitedly says.

"Yeah my Uncle makes those pieces so I asked him to teach me."

"You made it yourself?"

"Well barely! It took 3 attempts and a lot of guidance." I laugh.

"Oh my god that is so sweet!" The joyful excitement in her voice has shifted to mature wonder. "This might be the best present I've got, people usually don't put that much thought into me, just slippers and socks, thank you."

"You're welcome! Do you want the other one now?"

"There's another one? Definitely!"

I hand her the small jewellery box and she pulls out the opal necklace. She lunges at me and hugs me tight repeatedly thanking me. I pull away and look into her eyes.

"Bunny, I lo-"

I'm cut off by a loud slamming sound from downstairs and voice echoing up through the house, that of an older woman. "BETHANY!"

Silence and Bunny's attention has left me, the shout comes again "BETHANY!"

She grabs her phone "She's calling my sister, she must be in her room." She says frantically unlocking her phone. A banging on her door "Bethany, food will be ready in 10 minutes."

"Ok Mum." Bunny replies in a deflated tone.

The cogs move slowly, piecing together the moment, and I realise. "Your name isn't Bunny?" I ask, like a child being told Santa isn't real.

"Well that isn't really a real name so I mean technically no but I chose that name so it is me now, same as the clothes I wear I'm choosing what represents me I guess."

It was obvious all along it couldn't be her real name, but the shattering of the illusion hurt all the same. Did it matter? Maybe. To know something so fundamental was a lie makes me worry what else is a lie.

"No I'm just surprised is all."

"What were you saying a second ago?"

"Bunny I have to see my Uncle soon I was only popping in."

"Oh." Her tone deflates. "Okay."

I don't know why it freaked me out so much, just that such a massive change to what I thought I knew has left me feeling on uneven ground and unsure of everything. Why hadn't she told me? Did she not care about me? I text my uncle as I briskly walk down the street, he had wished me a Merry Christmas earlier but I missed it, I returned the greeting and asked if I could see him today.

"Make yourself comfy mate, I'm preparing food that should stretch to serve you, if I had known you were coming I could have prepared." Damien hands me a glass of whiskey with ice.

"Yeah sorry it was a change of plans."

"Weren't you seeing your girlfriend today?"

"Yeah something odd happened."

A grievous look sparks onto my uncle's face as he looks at me with noticeable concern. "What odd thing?" He worldly asks.

"Just with her it's not that important really."

The look fades with a little relief and he tops up my drink a bit more, "Sorry buddy it can be tough. Love is a rocky road. Talking of which I baked a rocky road I thought I would have to devour alone, care to help?"

"Can we start now?"

He laughs and leads me off through the large oak doors into the kitchen. Sitting on the counter top is a small pile of presents, unwrapped. "Aha I thought I'd hide them out here for you. Oh shit I have some mulled wine, it's been sitting around for years, wanna try cooking it?"

My eyes fleet away from the objects and sparkle, "More than anything**.**".

Knock out

Boxing day hits me with all of it's force. The next morning I awake nursing one hell of a hangover, I realise I haven't drunk much the past few weeks and so my tolerance has dropped considerably allowing the whiskey and mulled wine to shock and lay waste to my system. I allow myself a while to just lie and complain in bed, grunting angrily at the wall. Although my suffering is somewhat my own fault I'm not in the game for blame so allow my wall to receive the brunt of it. Whilst furiously scolding my wall for my actions I ignore the notification chime of my phone several times before eventually conceding against the wall and pocketing my phone on the way to the kitchen. I grab the easiest mug I can access, no thought for cleanliness. I lean against the sink, fumbling to start the kettle and find my loyal tin of coffee beans. I launch myself from the sink to the fridge and retrieve the empty milk bottle from inside. I sigh loudly and close the fridge door with a disheartened bump of my head. I give myself a leisurely 5 minutes to rest my head against the door, oozing the chill from within. Through a great deal of complaining I get myself dressed and make my way down to the lobby. The sun glares far too bright through the double glass doors, forcing me to close my eyes and take a seat in one of the scruffy tarnished armchairs that once defined this apartment block as "A nice place". It is clear time killed any care for this place, and whoever once invested heart into it has now left it to die beside the road like a deer mowed down at night.

"Oh good morning Mr Terret!" I hear a familiar chirp echo about the lobby. I drag my eyes open long enough to see Mr Davis and his Alsatian gliding over towards me. "Good morning Mr Davis." I reply, not attempting to hide the groggy tone in my voice. He smiles in an over enthused manner, always unnaturally happy for such a shit life. "You have a letter in your box, I was just on my way up to let you know."

There had been no post for me yesterday, and there are no deliveries on boxing day, perhaps he is lying to make conversation, or finally off the deep end. I thank him and head down the hall towards the post quarters.

Sure enough, there in my box sits a crisp white envelope which simply says "Patric". No address, nor a "K" to be found meaning it was delivered in here personally, likely someone in the building or else an outsider would need to discover the door code. Perhaps this is just the next development in Mr Davis peculiar quirks, for as long as I've known him there's been something odd I can't place my finger on. Of course I hardly know him, as mutual residents of this place I will occasionally pass him in the halls or lobby, or find myself trapped in the elevator with him, and yet when people are in your life they feel personal, even if you haven't formed a real connection with them. Perhaps that's just me, as

I find all the players in my life have importance regardless of proximity to events.

I Concede the war, heading back up to my apartment, white flag billowing at the day that has already beaten me. Once slumped in my homely green armchair I begin opening the letter. It's square and rigid so clearly a Christmas card, and yet I was deceived, upon pulling it out I'm greeted by a large orange pumpkin, grinning With fiery rage, and at the top "Trick or Treat" bounces out in bold orange letters. What the hell, Mr Davis must really have lost it now. I open it, praying for answers. But I only find more questions. 1 question. "If the owner of the horse is murdered, and the murderer claims the horse, how long can he perceive loyalty from the beast before it turns?"

At the bottom of the card is a small diagram of a horse kicking a stick man in the head. I don't recognise the handwriting or understand the joke. Rather than allowing trivial things to play on my mind, I condemn the card to the bin and continue struggling on with my day. I know that I will be forced to face Bunny at some point today, no way I'll get lucky enough to postpone it. To serve as a keen reminder, my phone continues igniting with notification lights, but I keep allowing myself 10 more minutes before reclaiming the reigns of responsibility. I'm finally coaxed back when the vacant black box of my screen is ignited like a phoenix rebirthing from the ashes my passion finds it's place back in my heart as Bunny's shy smile allures me from the caller ID.

"Hello, I'm sorry I've been groggy and sleeping all morning, just saw my phone going off."

A Tone I'm unfamiliar with takes me by surprise from Bunny, "Oh, that's okay, like are you okay?"

"Yeah I'm sorry, just a bit too much to drink at my Uncle's, I'm okay honestly."

"Are we okay?"

I can't reply. I know there's a problem and it annoyed me. I don't know why though, a part of me thinks it was just a reaction and isn't justified so I should just drop it.

If I just drop it and accept it then we can both be happy with no need for further disagreement which is what I want, right? But why should I have to drop something like this. Am I being needlessly defensive.

"Pat, are you still there?"

"Yeah I'm sorry, we're okay, I love you."

"I love you too." She sings back, relief apparent in her voice. "Do you want to go get something to eat?"

"It's basically still Christmas so good luck finding somewhere."

"Actually I have table reservations already, it's up to you if you wanna use them."

"Really? How?" I ask.

"Don't you remember?"

I don't.

An hour later I'm embracing Bunny with open arms, dressed to impress in a 3 piece suit, a mix of browns and burgundy. Her reservations were for an alarmingly expensive looking French restaurant named Trop tôt, housed inside a gorgeous Georgian building with excessively high ceilings inside, the environment gives me a sense of comfort, as I often visited much older grand houses with my uncle when I was just a boy. Bunny is looking stunning in a blue velvet dress. Once inside, settled at our table and into our drinks, Bunny begins telling stories like always, unlike always though I find myself quite amused by the tales. I notice myself enjoying the conversation too much, and feeling uneasy with this change I divert attention to the menu.

"What are you considering? What can you read?"

"This says French Dinning."

"Yeah in English though."

"Oooh well you should have specified what language! Well this says Pan."

"That's also English."

"True! But it's also French for bread. That's the full extent of my French."

I let myself succumb to her charm and just enjoy myself. Not so much a conscious choice, but the pleasure she creates in my mind has inflated, consuming and crushing all the problems hiding at the back.

"This is nice, we should do this more often!" I declare, intoxicated in the moment.

"Oui oui!" She replies, giving me a crafty look, resulting in me laughing into my drink. She looks at me sweetly a second before the sweetness subtly drained away, replaced by an extremely cautious look. "I'm sorry about the other day Patrick, I guess it was my name thing that set you off. I'm still the same person so I don't see why."

"So I can't be hurt?" I immediately defend. But for no reason.

"No I'm saying I can't apologise and help until understand why you're hurt, I'm not in validating your pain I'm trying to understand it."

"I'm sorry Bunny that was too defensive of me. I think the problem I have is it kinda made me feel I couldn't trust my world, I felt so certainly about how I felt about you and who you are, but that made me feel like I don't know you and I can't trust you."

She nods thoughtfully and takes my hand from across the table. "In my world my name is Bunny, so you any everyone else meet her first. I understand I should have been the one to tell you, maybe earlier, it's not a big deal to me though so I didn't think to. I trust you."

Such a mature and fair response from someone that has hurt me is rare, but then again so was my honest answer. "I think the problems we have are natural, I think together we can overcome them."

"I agree!" She chirps, holding her glass up to toast me. I clink my glass against hers and take a sip, taking a second to glance around the room. I had been so focused on Bunny that I hadn't noticed the affluent restaurant was hosting a wedding celebration at it's centre. About 40 people crammed around 3 tables right beside the live orchestra. Whilst all the guests were cheerily munching through their meals, the newly wed couple had taken the stage and begun waltzing with their respective worlds. The husband, a tall strong man with glasses and tidy hair, spins his new bride in a well synchronized display. Her long blonde hair whips around, golden in the lights, and concluding her spin, her hands re-join her husbands. They look into each other's eyes smiling warmly. I look back toward Bunny, who's gaze had also gone to the newlyweds hot footing around the dancefloor.

We smile warmly.

As the weeks go by

Zoo

Due to fear of things becoming stagnant and boring, me and Bunny have started going on at least 1 "interesting date" a week. This week was my choice and I hate choosing so I've brought her to the zoo. An easy choice and no girl can complain about cute and exotic animals so I'm hoping this will work out in my favour. Bunny/Beth seems excited now that we've stepped out of the lobby into the grand expanse full of pens containing animals otherwise fiction to our limited experiences. She excitedly runs to an enclosure containing a small pond inhabited by several cold looking flamingos doing nothing. Unable to fly.

"THEY'RE SO COOL" she exclaims. "Fuck, imagine being that pretty and pink"

I run my fingers through her hair "You already are"

"That's purple dummy"

My fingers move their way to her shoulder instead, deflated a little I say "Well I guess I won't try being nice again"

She spins around and pulls my arm across her back enveloping her in a hug, "Oh come on grumpy pants I said dummy, I was only joking. Thank you for bringing me here, for showing me all these rare animals being kept in slavery." She looks up at me laughing. I'm not laughing, but I do agree with her. Although this place allows me to see creatures I would never have otherwise seen for real, it does so by bringing them out of their home's, taking their freedom, and putting them in glass boxes like trophies. "This place used to make me so happy" I start "When I was a kid I guess I didn't know better, I felt more like I was meeting these animals than seeing them presented in depression and fear. It's easier to find joy in others if you ignore their needs and suffering." At this point Bunny/Beth doesn't matter, I'm providing myself therapy by expressing my feelings out loud, something I'm not entirely used to.

"Dude stop staring off in the distance, this a cool date and I appreciate you being sweet and bringing me here. My little sweet treat" She kisses my cheek and rubs her cold nose against it. She gets pulled into my coat by a hug and vigorously rubs her nose into it to warm it up. "Should we go into one of the indoor enclosures where it's a bit warmer?" I suggest.

By the time we get to the bat hall she has one of her earphones in, but I don't think I've done anything to annoy her. Perhaps she's bored. No she still seems adorned with the animals. I hold her waist from behind as we shuffle through the dark watching the silhouettes of bats fluttering behind the glass lining the wall. She's buoyantly bobbing her head from side to side and trying to follow the bats with her line of sight , made nearly impossible with them vanishing into the obsidian darkness. "Oh groovy!" she suddenly calls out and grabs my hand, pulling me into the next room, dancing through the dark. Laughing, she leads me to the aye-aye window "I can't even see it" she murmurs, her face pushed up against the glass. I tap the information board next to it with an artist rendition of an Aye-aye staring out "But with eyes like that I bet he can see you right now" She grits her teeth and widens her eyes, a pantomime reaction, "Well that's pretty creepy when you put it like that" She spins to the exhibit behind her. Behind the glass a single bulb dimly illuminates a few branches, from one hangs the shaggy fur of a sleeping sloth. "Aha! Imagine being able to be that lazy, sleeping all day and no one saying otherwise"

"You do sleep all day" I reply

"And you say otherwise" she retorts

"Fair point, I guess Sid is just lucky"

She shoots me a confused look, "Who's Sid?"

I point to the Sloth, "He is" I say. She scans the information board "How do you? Where does it say?" She asks.

"Oh it doesn't, we're just friends and I guess he only tells his friends his name" She stands silent for a second before erupting into laughter. "Oh my god Patrick, I was so thrown off, you're the last person I'd expect to name an animal"

I guess I am, "I didn't name him. I think he chose it himself" At this her laughter settles down to an almost self conscious level and she hugs me. As my head rests next to hers I hear that song we danced to muffled from her earphones.

A quiet night in

"If you had to name a baby what would you pick?"

"I don't think anyone would ever be stupid enough to let me do such a thing."

Bunny raises her head from my lap to look at me with faux puppy dog eyes, "I'm stupid enough to maybe."

I laugh as a shudder slides my spine. Surely not.

"You don't have one needing a name do you?"

"Of course I don't already have one!"

Oh god was that use of present tense a conscious choice. "You're not expecting to either are you?"

"Oh Gosh no time soon no! We have a whole future ahead of us, and I expect one day, a life might come from our love." Bunny says this, resting her head back on my lap. A single tear falls to her cheek from above. A startling amount of different emotions have awoken. Believing for that half a second that I was about to receive such life changing news started my head down an unfamiliar route. Perhaps it was my own lack of parents but I'd never really thought about being one. Although I felt the expected fear, that I don't want that responsibility, as the last thing I want to do is fail my child because I'm too young. But on the other hand the concept of meeting a living being we had created through love, that bridged any remaining gap between the 2 of us lit a beacon of hope in my heart. Positive emotions I don't recognise or can name flooded through me and still reside bubbling in my stomach. A shocking amount of disappointment and loss is alarmingly bouncing about my brain.

"You still didn't answer me!!" Bunny reminds me "Boy first!"

I have no answer so a joke is my escape "Patrick."

"Oh no surprise! Ya know that's a great name for a boy" She jokes, "What about a girl then?"

"Bethany."

Bunny looks at me shocked for a second, eyes inflated in a way I hadn't seen before. She let out an unrecognisable noise that I think is a good thing, before saying "That was way too easy for how smooth it came across. I love you." She cuddles into me and I smile, my heart still running rampant.

The Wildlife

Bunny is forcing me to perform in front of her friends today. After telling many stories about me and building an example I could never hope to fulfil I feel the weight of this coming social interaction. Since waking I've been overcome with an overwhelming sense of panic and dread. I feel ill but I know it's motion sickness from the shaking of a coward. A minor break in the stress inflicting my mind is discovered hiding in the corner of my room, a forgotten bottle of whiskey, still half full. It comes with me to the kitchen so I can make my second coffee of the day, this time with an Irish twist. As it cools on the counter I take a small bottle of coke from the fridge and drink about a quarter of it at once. I replace the missing amount with whiskey and return it to the fridge. I take a seat beside my buzzing phone and begin drinking my coffee.

"Oh good I finally woke you up!" Bunny cheers through the phone.

"Yay." I reply.

"This is Taylor, Jordan, Alex, Jo, and Stav! Don't trust Alex whatever you do but maybe if Jordan is involved but that'll involve Taylor too and well you'll understand, where's Z?" Unsure if I should reply or be quiet I wait a second for her question to be answered before nodding to the group of nameless individuals bubbling oozing individuality as if a poster desperately trying to sell the merits of another generic work. "I don't even know if Z's coming today, you know how difficult it is to contact them." One of the heard replied, burning neon plastic blazing from their hair. I insert my nod and "Hey" before withdrawing from the situation into my mind. I let the performance play silently in the background as I focus on more important affairs. My sleep has been far more rough recently, a great struggle to sleep, and an even greater one to stay in dream. Nightmares have always plagued me but they feel so much more real and ruthless now, enough to jolt me back into the waking world.

"Isn't that right Patrick?"

"Yeah." I hope it was right, or my tone carried enough dry sarcasm to get away with not hearing the question. I don't notice any distinct or major noises come from the group so I think I got away with it. No one seems to care that it's raining is that normal? It's lucky that I decided to bring my coat so I can hide within it, like a shell. An old camera is pulled out and the circus starts playing about taking probably very fun pictures that get spat out the bottom of the thing. One of them calls for one to be taken of me and Bunny. I smile and wave up my hand to reject the offer but Bunny excitedly hurries over to me, and I decide I can survive it. Bunny didn't remember a coat so her hair is all wet and matted, but she does look so happy. We smile and I'm blinded for a few moments. The large blots in my vision clear as Bunny comes back to me with a small square picture in her hand. The camera and direct light brought out all the worst features of my face. "Do you want it?" She asks slowly.

"Would you like to keep it?" I ask smiling.

"Thank you! I'd love to."

Thankfully, within an hour we're in a local pub, a chance to numb the surroundings further. I get 3 whisky and coke's so Bunny can have one too. Sadly the more comfortable environment relaxes a member of the group enough to begin recounting stories about people I don't know in events I couldn't care less about. I nod and sip my drink. The story manages to branch into another of equal disinterest and I gulp my drink. After a few more minutes not and feigning disbelief I excuse myself to the toilet, giving myself an opportunity to secure another drink. I allow myself 5 minutes in the toilet before returning to the bar for a drink and eventually dragging myself back to the table. Bright coloured beacons glowing so no one can miss them. We're all unimportant to the world, I think it's the brash choice to try and fight that which angers me most. I've accepted how small and insignificant my place is why haven't they. In 80 years we will be equal, dust in the same earth. Jesus maybe I should speak to someone other than myself when drunk. But the police branch earlier reaching my way had now snapped into a new energetic conversation elsewhere I couldn't hope to penetrate. As for Bunny, her attention has been absent since we arrived, payed as much care as her shadow. Why bother bringing me against my will to not acknowledge me?

She turns to me. "Are you okay sweetie?"

Anger and shame swell up inside me, sloshing amongst the alcohol. "Yes thank you, I'm just going outside for some cold air." I stroll towards the door, not bothering to grab my coat, feeling the sparks of anger attempting to ignite the shame in me. Since it's still January I soon come to regret this brash choice. Making the best of the situation I attempt to use the icy cold to ground myself. At that moment something heavy falls on my shoulders softly. My hands shoot up and grab the edges of my coat, as I turn to see one of them smiling at me and lighting a cigarette. "Thought you might need it!" They chuckle, punctuated by clicks of their lighter.

"Thanks." I reply.

"You smoke?" They ask, shaking the box towards me.

I raise my hand to shake them away but hesitate, raising my eyes to their beaming smile. I take one and return the smile.

In only an hour I feel fine amongst the crowd, now out on the dark streets, processing our way through an endless supply of drinks, I feel an odd rare energy, almost alive. The consuming fog of the daily slumber felt lifted, clear cool air is all that remains. There's a cat with such perfect energy looking at me from atop a brick wall. Looking, slightly wary, at the crowd bulldozing by. I stop to try and charm the little guy but he simply looks down at me with judgment. A traffic cone is kicked over. Beer is so odd, it tastes so rough and bitter but satisfying and homely, much like coffee, maybe that's the reason for this nostalgic tingle bubbling in me as the lights of the street blur across my gaze and my eyes turn up towards the everlasting sky above. A traffic cone is thrown into a garden. The group quickens pace, laughing without feeling the need to run. Wait Bunny is here, I almost forgot I was connected to events, rather than an audience member to this bizarre set of performances. She's drunk and laughing amongst the sea of alcohol coursing her veins. I approach her put my hand on her arm, "I love you." I softly say, blushing heavily she replies in kind and kisses me, to the loud response of our audience. She walks wrapped around my arm for a little while, telling wild stories I'd never heard before of plans I'd never heard before. "You want to be a journalist?" I reply at one point.

"Yeah, since I was young."

"You don't even read the paper. Do you know anything about writing?"

"Why are you being mean?"

"I was intending to sound mean at all I'm surprised and confused, I'm probably a bit afraid, being a struggling writer, that you might outdo me at the only thing that gives me value."

"You idiot." She says, hugging me.

A bin is kicked over into the road, contents gushing across the street.

We all cheer.

Someone throws a rock at an old teacher's house and we all run, laughing.

I empty the remains of my bottle into my mouth. The empty bottle smashes against the brickwork of number 61, showering shards of glass down onto the front garden. The group exclaims .

"Holy shit!"

"I can't believe it!"

Another bottle is tossed from the group.

"Fuck you Nigel."

The group runs off laughing and I stay stood at his front gate. Almost a month and I had heard nothing from him. I did however, hear his dad had been released from prison this month, perhaps staying here wasn't the best option. Neither was picking up the large stone from the street. Neither was hurling it at a front window. I now conform to the group and begin running, blood pumping something else around my veins. As if something alive is spreading through my body I feel changed, enhanced.

At a safe distance the group laughs hysterically over proceedings, and stories of other stupid choices come out. These stories switch topic to Nigel.

"Oh my god what was the play wasn't it something really crap?" A green head asks.

"Oh god no that was awful! It was Romeo and Juliet!" Bunny replies.

"That's the worst possible play they could have given you!" Roars a shaved head.

"What's wrong with Romeo and Juliet?" I ask, not quite aware of the topic.

"That guy who's house you bottled used to be obsessed with Bunny in college, then they had to work together on a performance piece and they were given parts of Romeo and Juliet. Obviously he made sure he was Romeo, and as gorgeous talented actress naturally Bunny was Juliette."

Bunny blushes and poses her face.

My face also fills with blood. It burns my cheeks.

"And then obviously that drove him mad he thought they really were together and well what a psycho."

Everyone laughs. I stare at the far corner of the park, shrouded in darkness. I look past the darkness, through the houses that presumably stand beyond it, and directly at Nigel. This had been the explanation for everything. I'd been swirling around trapped in a whirlpool of confusion.

The rest of the night levels out and loses momentum, we vacate the park and return to the streets, some voicing their decision to head home soon. The energy re-sparks a little though when a car with a pro life sticker in the window gets a key across it's paint. Everyone chuckles and commends them, but less so than before. I'm still steaming with anger, bubbling to the brink. Somebody spits on a political poster.

A car catches my attention. I can't register why at first, but it glints and calls to me. Then Dejavu starts creeping over me, until it slots into place. I've been in it before. A long time ago, or so it feels, me and Natalie sat in the back of Jason's car on the way to Indigo Cliff. Jason's car.

Not yet returning from my mind, my body strikes out, smashing the bottle in my hand against the side of the car. I feel small shards slice through the skin of my hand, showering outwards. My mind returns to feel this and swiftly exits. The crowd mixes gasps and cheers, as my key comes out of my pocket and into the side of the car, scratching deep gashes down it, my hand leaking red as I do so. Fate left a copper pipe just beside the street for me which I retrieve before running at the car, cleaning it of it's wing mirror and finally setting off the alarm dispersing the group. I remained. I wasn't finished with the windscreen, upon which I plant a beautiful large crack. No one comes.

I stand panting beside the screaming car.

I calm a little with each breath, I look over to see Bunny and the group looking at me horrified.

"What the fuck" They say.

Milkshake

Bunny meets me on the way home from work and we detour to grab coffee, an attempt to warm our tired minds on a drizzly March afternoon. Our plans came to a crash with the door locked and the lights off. "Well that's odd it's only half four, it's usually open much later." I try the door again with no hope for success.

"Well there's that milkshake place I keep suggesting, that's only 5 minutes down the road" The milkshakes are a terrifying price and so I keep disregarding this suggestion from Bunny but that doesn't stop her bringing it up every time I see her. "That's not really coffee" I complain.

"Oh come on you know how bad I want to go, why cant we do something for me?" Her volume rises.

"This place is cheap and convenient, that's like 5 minutes out of my way and it's cold I don't want a cold drink" I can sense this escalating, but with the stress of the day I can't stop myself.

"Alright dick, I'll go solo" apparently neither can she

"Bunny please wait, let's not do this, let's just get milkshake you're right" I concede. She shoots me a suspicious glance, eyes tight.

The building is tall and has a wooden facade making it look like an elongated ski hut. "This is incredible! Can we sit upstairs?"

"Why is there an upstairs in a milkshake shop?"

"So you can look down on people with your art-ees-ian milkshake" She puts major emphasis on the "ees" part.

"That's not how you pronounce it, it's arti-san"

She throws her hand to her hips "Well then you're an idiot because that is how I pronounce it. English is subjective"

I walk past her and roughly push open the glass swing door. The rustic decor outside is juxtaposed by a white, teal, and pink interior looking to resemble a 70's diner.

The prices certainly don't resemble the 70's, "£6.50 for one?? How is it worth that much" I loudly exclaim, drawing the attention of staff and patrons alike.

"Thanks for ruining this for me too" Bunny quietly remarks beside me, walking up to the till looking ashamed to order hers. Perhaps insecurity caused my outburst but I hardly think it's fair on Bunny, so I quickly head to the till and offer to pay for both.

"Sure it's not too much for you?" asks the guy at the till, not tall, not much older, a stupid beard. I physically bite my tongue and my smile, holding out my card to pay.

We sit upstairs at Bunny's request, at a window seat overlooking a fairly uninteresting and quiet street. "What an excellent view of all the other buildings" I exclaim with sarcasm. Bunny smiles then looks at me and stops, apparently unaware of the sarcasm. "Well everyone downstairs saw you being a asshole" she sighs staring at the low level of traffic below. I wasn't an asshole, the prices are unbelievable and I was just saying, I'm sure they all agreed with me. I continue my justification train whilst staring at the top of her head as she gazes out the window, head slumped. Her roots are starting to show through, and actually quite bad now that I can see this angle, I wonder if she knows. "Your roots are showing" I say.

"Oh fuck off" she snaps, scowling at me, "I just wanted to go on a nice date to a nice place with my nice boyfriend"

Shit. Nice place though? "You chose wrong for that"

"Yeah I forgot to invite my nice boyfriend" Bunny spent the rest of the drink on her phone.

Upon departing the shake place I take some time to reflect on Bunny's perspective of events. She was probably just excited to take someone she liked somewhere she liked, and I guess I ruined both for her by moaning. If I had made it more of a joke I could have let out my frustration whilst not making it obvious and spoiling the mood. Or am I just overthinking things? "Look I'm sorry, I think I understand why you're upset" I call to her, walking just a little in front of me, absorbed on her phone. "Do you?" she spins aggressively to face me, pocketing her phone for the coming fight "I don't think you understand me at all, do you even understand yourself? You switch from so lovely to so vile so quickly that I don't think you're even a person just a puppet to your emotions. I wish I knew what was in your head when you spoil everything but I doubt I could even comprehend the toxic spew. In fact I doubt even you can comprehend what's in that fucked up skull." The aggression breaks and a heavy sob is released. Am I really that bad? Her loud outbreak has turned heads and was a little over the top causing a defensive rigidity in me, "Bunny, what are you talking about?"

She glowers at me, eyes teary and red "Leave me alone" she hisses through grit teeth before storming off in the direction of her house. I don't get it.

I get it

Uncle Damien is celebrating his 42nd birthday with a gathering in his sizeable, ancient house. I invited Bunny, thinking it would be a nice environment to spend time together in. After all she seems desperate to gentrify herself, and Damien's place is furnished with lavish decor ranging from the 1800's to about the 1980s' at which point I think interior design took a turn he couldn't appreciate. It makes for an interesting if not beautiful environment. After explaining this Bunny seemed somewhat on board, then out of the blue cancelled. After much back and forth over the last week she agreed, yet here I am waiting for her 2 hours after we had agreed. She won't even answer her phone and I don't want to leave my flat in case she does turn up. Sitting here in my old armchair I'm stewing in my anger, a mask to conceal my worry. Nothing would have happened to her surely, it's just a normal day. Maybe she's cheating on me, or just passed out in a dingy front room, her system pumped full of alcohol or drugs. I spend some time with the pad and pen clutched in my hand, but no inspiration comes to me and the page remains blank. I make a coffee for myself loudly exclaiming "What a bitch" and "She'd better be alright " between pouring the milk, sugar, and whiskey. Carrying my coffee back to my chair I see my phone light up, causing me to rush over and spill a little coffee on the floor. "Dammit" I exclaim, typing Bunny52 into my password box. The phone unlocks and displays her message. "Hey, sorry. I'm awake now"

No explanation for her absence I'm left to guess how she slept so late for so long. Delayed by my processing of events, she sends a second message before I can reply. "I'll be there in 20 minutes, if you're still home"

Whatever, getting to the party is still my priority and so I swallow my frustration and reply telling her to meet me halfway in 10 minutes and I dash out.

I get there first and she arrives only a few minutes later, drained of colour aside from the dark bags beneath her eyes, unsuccessfully masked beneath a thin layer of makeup. I also recently noticed Bunny has been letting her roots run rampant, combined with the ill look on her face makes her look as if she's dying. She walks slowly towards me, vacant at first, but upon noticing me she fakes a pained smile to me, closing her eyes as she does. "Hey" She murmurs, moving straight in to hug me.

"You look terrible, how fucked up did you get last night?"

She pulls away and looks at me with a sense of pained confusion, amplified heavily by her gaunt appearance. "What's wrong with how I look?"

"You look like you drank too much and slept too little, although you managed to sleep through this. Although I imagine you weren't sleeping."

Rather than the barrage of insults and arguments I was expecting to receive in response, there is instead an unnerving silence. I dare to look her back in the eye and see the genuine pain on her face. I can feel so much anger, why isn't she reciprocating it, why isn't she sparking more from me and entering a cycle of stoking each others fires until the weakest gets burned first and retreats.

"Is it that noticeable?" She finally asks.

I have all this anger and no fair place to put it, trying to hold it down I answer, "No, you just look ill and I guess I would notice more than some."

"I am ill. I'm sorry I kept you waiting so long I was feeling too bad to get up and get my phone."

I feel the molten rage in me simmering and churning unsure where to go. If I had been ill and Bunny forced me to meet new people I would have stayed at home. Am I selfish for staying home, or am I selfish for dragging her now. "What's wrong? Do you feel well enough to be out?"

"Yeah I'm sure I'm fine now. It was just like a fit, maybe a massive panic attack or something. I was kind of stuck on the floor for a bit and kind of lost track of time." There's a hurried uncertainty to her words I've never really heard before, as if speaking on impulse rather than thought.

The molten in me cools from inactivity and the recollection of the suffering panic attacks caused me, and in fact how Bunny had helped me when I needed it. Of course she did make me do things I didn't want to though and I did. This negative thought sweeps into mu my mind and I make a conscious effort to swipe it back out of my mind, calming myself again. "I didn't know you were effected by them, I'm sorry."

"I'm sorry I let you down"

"You haven't, you're right here."

She weakly smiles at me, "I know how important your uncle is to you, I'm sorry you could have gone on I wouldn't have minded."

"I think I was just very worried about you, more so than missing my uncle's party. I'm not sure, I thought I was angry but now I just feel relief." I feel a weird mix of weakness and relief wash over me at this admittance, decanting my armour is dangerous but life will surely be easier.

"Maybe more of you anger is based on fear and you don't realise it, maybe you will be able to now." Bunny observes as if I'm but a glass sculptor boasting all.

I fight the defensive response kicking off in my body, wanting to defend and argue and protect myself from vulnerability. To move me safely into any state other than vulnerable. But she's likely giving sincere advice and not trying to dig, so I swallow it down as best as I can. "Yes hopefully." I hurriedly say before switching away from the difficult topic. "How are you feeling now? You look like standing is a struggle."

"I'll be okay." She lies.

My uncle is incredibly understanding and fair, he's not superficial enough to care about a party. I was hoping for everyone to see how beautiful Bunny was, and the depth of her care for me, but they'll all get another chance.

"No, come on, you need to rest, I don't want to risk you feeling any worse." I say with certainty, placing a reassuring hand on her shoulder.

Tears visibly fall down her face. "I don't want to ruin you or your Uncle's day."

"It's okay he will understand. And no day in which I see your smile can be ruined."

She hugs me and begins leading me back to my flat.

She still plays that she's fine despite visibly struggling to stand and talk. I sit her down in the comfort chair and begin grabbing blankets and preparing hot drinks. We sit talking about hair colours and other comfort topics like chocolate. After about an hour of mindless chat she shifts topics heavily, "That was quite impressive earlier Patrick. To re-evaluate your feelings after they'd already formed. I was nervous so I was watching you closely and I could see you fighting with your own feelings to put mine first. I appreciate it."

I sit quietly sipping my tea, still somewhat a stranger to self scrutiny. This big vulnerable hole through which my feelings are visible feels like a wound, but I know it is more than necessary. "You're welcome." I quietly reply over my tea.

The party bustles with life, an antique room decorated with antique people engaging in cheery conversation and sharing deep laughs. Through the crowds of well dressed acquaintances glides it's host, Damien. With two tall glasses of white wine in hand he makes his way up to a woman looking to be in her mid 40's, short brown hair with a tint of ginger. "Special delivery." Damien beams, handing her a glass.

"Oh thank you, running the party and the catering?"

"I'm a man of many talents." He coolly says, sipping his own glass.

"Oh he's arrived by the way, I saw him walking into the other room just a second ago." The lady points towards a cracked open large oak door behind which the party had spread. "Oh I didn't think he could make it? He doesn't usually come to social gatherings." He smiled and gave a slight bow of his head before dashing off into the next room, spilling a little wine on the lapel of his suit. Thankfully he hadn't opened the bottle of red.

Upon entering the next room he was immediately greeted with the guest in question. A difficult man to miss, tall with strong dark features and wild hair, dressed in an exquisite 3 piece suit. They both spot each other at the same moment, a grin spreads across both their faces. Damien hurries over to him, extending a hand to shake, an invitation accepted. "So glad you could make it, have you had a drink yet? I just opened an excellent bottle in the kitchen."

"Not yet, you'll have to take me there Pisces, I love a vintage."

Damien's head shoots around the crowd, "Quite a few of the guests aren't from work so if you can just say Damien?"

The guest let's out a quiet deep chuckle, "Whoops, my bad."

The two men walk their way through the crowd, guests moving to let them through with ease.

The guest takes a few glances around the crowds, "So Patrick couldn't make it?" He asks, draining some white wine from his glass.

"Uh no he couldn't, girl problems."

The guest let out a knowing chuckle, "We've all been there. Have you mentioned the order to him?"

Damien stops, hand paused on the kitchen door. "No, after what he's been through there's no way I'm bringing him into this, he's not like Michael's boy, not as strong minded, and he's not even my son."

The guest raises his hand to the door and pushes it open from Damien's, making his way into the kitchen he says, "He might as well be."

Big trouble in little hearts

Since the event before my Uncle's party Bunny has been acting strange. I haven't seen her for almost a week since it happened and contact has been scarce, seemingly always busy. I'm confused I thought I handled the situation right and fairly so why am I suffering from the outcome? Perhaps I was too nice to her, maybe she's so used to being mistreated by the world that turning nice scared her off. I mean I always tried to treat her right, never knowingly hurting her, but I guess our ideas of relationships and interactions are poisoned by those around us and I can't name a friend that's had a healthy relationship. Well I can't name a friend full stop now. Thinking I was always putting quality above quantity it seems no one can really be trusted. Maybe quantity is the way to go, back up friends in case frontrunners fall through. I just feel worthless and non existent on account of things.

When I finally catch Bunny's attention long enough to hold a conversation I take my chance to address the perpetuating situation and it's effects on me. She apologises and suggests meeting me in a few hours, without hesitation I agree.

I rest my legs over the side of the bridge, swaying in the wind. Below my dangling feet sits 300 feet of nothing, the absence has weight somehow. Yet sitting here, knowing I have the choice, makes me feel a lot better. Knowing that I will never be forced to endure the suffering of life without being able to conclude it myself gives me some feeling of power in a powerless moment.

Things went wrong in record time.

"Should we go somewhere nicer? The middle of the city is gross." A good suggestion from her, perhaps a calmer setting of scenery could have produced a calmer discourse. Sadly I was unable to control myself long enough to not destroy my dreams, delicate as a glass house, shattered beyond repair by my impish mind.

Across this crowded moaning bridge, overstuffed with vehicles chugging out toxins into the air, the environment broke my restraint and my mind and mouth ran amok.

"Where the hell have you been? Why have you left me in the dark??"

I watch the final beams dance through the clouds on the horizon as the sun resigns his place in the sky for the day. The burning gas giant allowing the floaty rock to take centre stage in the sky, backlit by a million dead galaxies, long dead but leaving in their death only a beautiful light to guide through the endless dark. Space is weird.

"Look Patrick I've had a lot happen can we not just wait until we get somewhere nicer?"

"Oh I bet there was but I wouldn't know, you want me to wait even longer for answers?"

My gaze dips down past my feet to the infinite drop beneath. A deep river runs beneath the bridge, and given recent weather the flow is running with extreme force, crashing around rocks and reforming to continue it's journey forward. Regardless of obstacles the water always runs towards the same goal, the big collective in the ocean, only to be evaporated and rained back to the start. I find comfort applying this idea to life. We start at birth, and go through a path decided by external forces, like pawns of time we travel ever forward, never backward. And if my Hope's are well placed when everything ends it can start again.

"I don't know where I want to take my life!"

"Oh a future with me is no longer good enough?"

"Well if you're always going to be like this!"

"LIKE WHAT??"

I should have learned from previous arguments. I should have held myself to a higher level. I let

Bunny down. I let myself down. At least she can be happy now.

"Do you even know what I want to do with my life?" Her question had caused so much shame I retreated into a further position of defence.

"You can't even be honest about your name why would I bother listening to anything you say?" My response visibly hurt her, her tone switches to reflect that and it made me feel so much more shame.

"It's a new year, by October I could have achieved my goal, but all you're going to do is hold me back."

Feeling completely crushed but unwilling to give up fighting I could only mock her. "Ooooh new year, new me." I sarcastically mock her tone. Idiot.

"No more of this!"

"Of course I'm discarded now"

"Don't always make this about you. I shouldn't have expected any less when I need you. I'm done." She storms off. She is gone. Bunny is lost. I take my seat on the side of the bridge and begin trying to find a new world.

It's dark now, very few people have walked past but the cars are still fairly frequent but reduced in number. Time to leave I think, no need to cause Bunny more pain. My uncle who has always supported and loved me, what a waste it would be. I owe it to them at least to continue and make the most of myself. I gave too much faith to someone capable of consolidating my soul and now I feel weak. Absent. I will return home, a home, not the desired one, with my head hung low.

Whilst traipsing home I combat the intrusive recollections of the argument. So much unnecessary anger, there was so little communication just pointless attempts to one up and blame. We both failed us. There is no value the aggressive parts, nothing achieved or conveyed. I might as well forget the whole thing.

I probably have medicine for this pain at my apartment. I'll be better soon.

I can live without Bunny.

Bunny can live much happier without me.

Does Venus burn bright in the fall?

Thump-Thump.

Things are fine.

Thump-Thump

I'm okay. By October I will have achieved my dreams and this will all be over.

Thump - *thump*

I guess this is just a side effect of going cold turkey. In fact that was likely the cause last week as well.

Thump.

Fuck. I wasn't cold turkey it was just one day without. Even still, I will be fine. I have a goal, first time in a long while, a goal for myself.

Thump-Thump

A new life for a new woman. I look into the mirror with pride, feeling more recognition than expected for the stranger before me. My hair tied up hiding the lavender tips, a final attachment to a time passed I'm not yet ready to cut. The rest of my hair has returned to chestnut which is pretty close to my natural colour, the closest thing to it I've seen in a long time. With this yellow jumper on as well it gives the appearance that the lavender has blossomed into a sunflower.

THUMP.

Is it skipping a beat or beating slow? Little matter I'll be fine after I've slept, I'm always fine. Focus on the now, not on the possible future. I look down at my art and readjust my priorities, focus on the future I can control, not the future beyond my control. An artist by the fall.

Thump.

I whimper a little and don't know why. I had put music on, but the vinyl has come to an end without my noticing and is now scratching out silence. Readjusting the needle I notice the small pile of Polaroids on my table next to the player. From the top of the pile Patrick's face smiles out, looking wild with excitement, his eyes on me, a mess of a girl cuddling into him with wet stringy purple hair covering squinting eyes and a sincere smile. I was happy. I can't be happy like that again though can I? Not in that way anyway. Maybe this is just a show as well, making desperate and extreme yet ultimately unnecessary decisions to find myself an identity.

Thump.

No this is different, this is to feel the appreciation and love I need from myself, not to source it from vulnerable idealists that give me a second glance. I don't want him, I want that stability back rather than the uncertainty change brings with it. I'm ready for change. Repositioning the needle, the album begins again. I pick up the top Polaroid and gently dance back towards the bed, allowing the joyous melancholy of the music to guide my movement leaving me free to wander in my mind instead. I listened to this album with him so many times, I am listening to it with him, all of those times, all now. I collapse onto my bed and lie on my back looking up at the poster on my ceiling. Patrick is inspecting it for the first time "Oh the Sistine chapel?" I whisper through quivering lips. But now my mind is seeing through eyes of the past. He's naming the sloth at the zoo. And this song, we're dancing at the house party, meeting in the market, I'm cradling him in the smoking area playing music on my phone to calm him. I'm with viola being played the song for the first time and feeling all these emotions that felt like memories. My first kiss with Tom, my first crush fever over Luke. A time when I was young and happy and safe tucked up in bed, full of optimism. My 10th birthday, all my friends and family surrounding me feeling inflated and full of power. The train track my parents got me for the divorce. My mum sitting me on her lap in the park, a much younger beautiful woman, holding her precious baby close to her as she rests on a bench at the top of the hill. It's October with skies grey and trees mere skeletons, I sit bundled up in my layers with my coat, scarf, gloves, and a woolly hat. The floor and bench are wet, with further rain expected soon. We sit looking out over the miles of city visible from so high. I look at mum and she looks back smiling "I love you sweet" she says. My blurry eyes fail to focus on the photograph of Patrick and Bunny. "I love you too" A whisper quiet enough to be lost in the wind.

The song ends.

Phobos

I feel nothing but the cold floor pressing against my body. Slowly I open my eyes, quickly reversing my choice as the light burns it's way into my vision. Even through my closed eyes the light burns so harshly filling my vision with the red of my blood. I keep my eyes screwed close and bury my head back into the floor, dimming the intrusive light. The floor feels unstable, as if drifting on a boat, I can feel my sense of balance going wild. Covering my head with my arms I attempt opening my eyes again. Although the shielded light is bearable, my eyes are unable to focus making me feel dizzy and queasy. I let my centre of gravity shift all around the place, sloshing the contents of my stomach. I quietly count to 10 before moving my arm allowing the light back in. Slowly I adjust to it and try raising my head to look around. I'm in my apartment, the middle of the living room. My armchair is overturned beside me, as if cradling me from behind. I imagine I had fallen asleep on it and an odd angle and tipped it. Razor pain repeatedly sheds it's way through my head in waves. Chess pieces scatter the floor, with a half empty bored still sitting on the table. My mind is just overwhelmed by the pain in this moment. I try standing, using the fallen chair as support, but am quickly defeated and find myself slumped against the chair. Breathing with great difficulty I scout about the room, empty bottles are scattered everywhere. No use to me now. I launch myself up from the armchair and stumble across the room, slamming into the wall for stability. Keeping my weight against the wall I lead myself along the wall to the door, through which I fall. The bathroom spins about me as I pull myself up using the sink, from the big glass box on the wall I see a vile mess of a man. Stubble starting to stretch across my face, my eyes dark and sunk, my skin pale and unhealthy. A few seconds is more than enough, I turn to the toilet and my sloshing stomach is ejected into and across the bowl. Through hours of struggle I brush my teeth, make my way to the kitchen, make a coffee, and finally collapse in the chair still standing. It's 3pm now, the day is in full swing. Where can I get tonight's medicine from? I need to sober up soon so I can make it outside and get drunk again. Each sip of the coffee burns a little awareness into my mind, and with these pangs of sense I get snippets of reality come back to memory I could feel her in my subconscious waiting to be remembered, and now the gates have opened I can't keep my mind from wandering to her. Something feels wrong today, thinking of her feels hollow, could this be the numbing of my feelings? It's a blur, but I'm not sure that I dreamed about her last night, the first time in the last 2 weeks, even more progress. I can't describe this feeling beyond possibly a strange sense of silence, but in my mind not my world. Something is wrong. I know I could feel her, we were connected beyond just our bodies, had the connection rotted now? Has that love run out?

I close my eyes and try drawing focus on my breathing, letting thoughts leak away giving me peace. My uncle always tried talking to me on a spiritual level when I was growing up, I was too young to give it my attention or absorb much but I put what I remember into practice. I let a memory of Bunny emerge in my mind a pay attention to every feeling it sparks. As my mind drifts on o keep hold of the feeling. "Bunny." I whisper beneath my breath.

I'm suddenly thrown out of calm concentration by the violent vibrating of my phone. Jolted into action I grab my phone, and answer in raspy voice "Hello."

A few seconds of silence.

"Is this Patrick?" A voice cautiously asks.

"Yes I am, who is this?"

"It's Alex."

"Who?"

"Bunny's friend, we met in the pub."

Oh god what's the meaning of this, my stomach lurches but I swallow down the desire to be sick again. "Oh right."

"I'm sorry, we didn't know who should tell you, but I guess I'm the bravest."

My heart pounds and I feel the beating drums of a panic attack marching towards me. I don't want to know what Bunny has done without me. "Tell me what?" I spurt out over jagged breaths.

"I'm sorry Patrick, Bunny passed away last night. She was in bed so they think she passed in her sleep."

Everything stops. My body turns to ice, all life and energy draining out, frozen solid. This is a fucked up joke.

"Look I'm sorry Patrick, we all know how happy you two were so this must be hard for you as well. We don't want you having to deal with this alone so if you need anyone you can reach out to any of us."

"I'm sorry." I begin. "I didn't try getting to know any of you enough when I had the chance. I don't deserve any of you trying to help me during this, you'll be struggling just as bad as me, and I'm certain I can't help any of you."

"Kindness is the key, being able to forgive is the most important thing people need to learn, we want to help you too."

"Thank you, but I can't forgive myself, I hope you all find happiness soon."

"Patrick please wait."

I hang up. Silently staring from my chair, unblinking, unthinking, numb. My phone rings a few times and beeps to notify me of a few texts. Support from her friends. I didn't just ignore them I actively disliked them for no reason. They're stupid to offer me help why the hell do they think I deserve it. Why the hell do they think they can forgive me. No one can forgive me.

Romeo steps forward

The days that followed felt unreal, with each day opening and closing without purpose. I lifelessly moved from one destination to another without purpose, sitting in silence around my apartment, park benches, and the coffee shop. Even my mind sits silent, not really processing events but sitting in silent surrender. As the scenery around me changed I remained unaffected, unflinching, a fixed gaze past the world around me. Perhaps an attempt to look beyond for answers but I have no certainty. And if so I was unsuccessful, no answers have become clear. My phone remains on silent, only occasionally checked between one limbo and another. A few messages and calls of concern but nothing needing my attention right now. That is until my phone suddenly recaptured all of my attention with a single surprise.

A text, a text from Nigel. I didn't expect any messages of sympathy from him, creating a small sense of doubt in the recess of my mind. I finish cleaning the remaining plates, dry my hands, and take a look. There is no message of sympathy, simply the words "Van-Damme drama academy" and the time 5:30pm. Wrong number? Then again he loves his silly games and this isn't too out of character. I check the old clock hanging on the wall. Just past 2pm. I have time to decide if I should ignore it or not. This isn't a puzzle that needs the full hours, I'm certain I'm going, even if it a mistake, this intrigue and painful pit in my stomach is the first thing I've felt since finding out. I'm very aware this will likely result in pain for me in some way, but at this point the sharp sting of pain is more desirable than this absence. I need to feel alive again, even if I have to walk into darkness to find any sense of feeling.

For the following hours I impatiently shift around my apartment, watching the hour hand fall so painfully slowly from 2 down to 3 finally to 4, at which point I couldn't bare it any longer and headed out. I remember where Nigel's old drama academy was, he can't help but point it out every time we would pass. So this is where Bunny met Nigel, and the host, without this catalyst we may never have met at that party. It's 4:35 and the sun is just about giving up, retreating behind thick clouds on the horizon, in darkness I arrive. I wait across the road from the old theatre, sitting out of sight on a bench. I keep a rigorous watch but I don't see Nigel approach from anywhere. The academy is built around the old theatre, A tired old Victorian building, half demolished. Comparatively cheap and modern expansions clash awfully against it, tastelessly shoved onto the old building to repurpose it for education.

At 5:02 I receive a text

"Tut tut Pat you let me down, late as ever."

"I'm outside." I reply.

"Well then come in."

All of the lights across the building are off and it's definitely not open hours, he must be messing with me, how and why is he inside. All the alarm bells in my head ring out and I feel a deep pit of fear in my stomach. Unwilling to lose the twang of life I feel inside, I stand from the bench and make my way to the lifeless building. Sure enough the gate is unlocked and hanging slightly ajar, as is the front door. I make my way inside and through mind numbingly dark halls, I know where to go, I know Nigel will be centre stage. A small slither of light crawls from beneath the double doors to the main hall, so without wasting a second I push through. I'm met with a large flat seating area with rows throughout leading up to the main wooden stage towering above. The doors slam behind me and I make my way up to the stage, scouting around the room. Music begins blasting from behind the stage, something operatic, but far too loud for the speakers to handle causing painful distortion.

A small section of the front of the stage is exposed with large purple velvet curtains drawn, masking the back half of the stage. Still cautiously looking around I take a seat in the second row from the front, waiting.

The overbearing music abruptly cuts out, and the curtains begin parting, racing to parallel corners. Out strides Nigel, his blonde curly hair an unkempt mess, dressed in contrast in a full suit. Tie and all. The suit is all black matching the tie, coupled with a plain white shirt. He grins at me with a level of contempt and desperation visible in his eyes.

"Oh you didn't dress up for me? I dressed up for you, but of course I never expect any courtesy from you." He gestures a vicious point at me.

"I didn't realise there was a dress code." I cautiously reply, unsure of the purpose of all this.

"Well of course not you were never presumptuous, always too afraid to form your own thoughts and opinions, too afraid to be wrong?" The jesters mocking tone makes me more uneasy, I'd rarely seen this level of bravado and direct spite used together by Nigel. A rare and concerning occurrence. "My fear of being wrong, of thinking for myself is what led me to make the worst mistakes, I'm now aware of that." I reply.

"Oh of course, you find clarity and all it cost was Bunny's life. Glad to see you reached enlightenment."

I feel the fires of rage begin to ignite in my stomach, sparked by his carefree mocking disregard for the loss of everything. I attempt to extinguish by reminding myself that this is the way Nigel has always dealt with pain, but it's of little success. All of this goes unnoticed as he continues indulging in his monologue, "So proud of you sweet child for reaching enlightenment, you only had to kill 2 people that loved you to achieve it. Oh bravo! And with all sincerity I hope the lone wolf finds better pray in which to sink your teeth." His act is accompanied by various over dramatized movements waving his hands for emphasis. Mine remain clenched inside my jacket pockets. I can tell he wants me to ask who the second is but I won't bite.

"Is this all because your dad got let out of prison? This isn't you."

"Ha! I've already dealt with my dad! After 8 years in prison there will always be people looking for you, I just had to tell them where to find him."

I don't believe what I'm hearing. Any hope of verbally retaliating diminishes as pain intoxicates my brain bursting into pain, the wound of his words deep enough already to elicit a fight or flight response to consume me. Violence never heeds a resolution just more anger and violence, perpetuating itself.

"Oh come on! This is too much like my lone rehearsals, I put such work into every aspect of tonight and you're standing there silent. Ask me!

You must have wondered, or has my performance fallen on deaf ears?"

"Not your best work."

"Well I did only have a day to prepare. I blame it on the audience, this crowd is dead." His eyes glide past me to the main door in a dead hanging stare, "Well, not yet. Oh the magic on this stage! Macbeth, Les Mis, and of course as you know Romeo and Juliet. An act you recently performed in fact, although frankly I think I was the better Romeo." He squats down on stage meeting my eye level in a hunched crouch, starring me down.

"I'm sorry." I say, maintaining eye contact.

An overplayed shock jumps across his face as he rocks back and falls into a sitting position, a painfully joyous look on his face, "Already? Aha! I didn't think I'd get that until things heated up a bit. Perhaps then sincerity rather than desperation? Maybe it's better, but I did want to hear the broken desperation. Hopefully it's still to come."

My senses are spiking preparing me for a flurry of a fight, but still desperate for peace a vulnerability in me is shouting at me to talk down this situation and end it as soon as possible. "There's no need to go on with anymore of this, I know you're hurt as well and I'll do whatever it takes to help you. But please come off that stage I don't think it's good for your head."

He just starts laughing at me, still sat lazily on the stage in front of me. "I hate it when things don't turn out as planned, I've never been great at improv'. Do I continue as close to the original plan as possible or do I embrace the new turn." He becomes visibly frustrated, "Damn why couldn't you be as simple as expected? Although I guess you were always pathetically apologetic I could of expected it. Should have prepared emotionally. I'm doing what I have to do, don't you see how unlikely all of this was? It's a story! If not, every story before has prepared me for this. It's all fiction. The coincidences, the uncharismatic protagonist who achieves every goal without struggle. Our lives aren't our own."

Sanity seems gone from him completely as he gazes directly at the spotlight burning the stage with it's glow. I feel hope die in me, I lose all faith in an easy resolution. My body heat has been rising throughout his speech, indicative of my anger consuming me as I endured his mournful performance. Suddenly his eyes snap back down to me, the rest of his body remaining frozen and still. "I never questioned who's story, I always assumed yours, but only the Gods have the power to play like this, perhaps some deity is playing with our paths for his amusement." His face contorts a little as he stands "Or to help us, difficult times create strong men, maybe we're being guided, maybe suffering is necessary."

The hot flush consuming me I'm losing patience for the nonsense being spouted, I begin to become aware that the heat is all around me, that this room is actually incredibly hot, it hadn't just been my anger burning up. Nigel suddenly leaps down from the stage, landing just beside me, he straightens himself and says "I'm sorry too, I guess we should get out of here."

"I'm glad you agree."

"I assure you it's not for the same reason." He solemnly says, throwing a handful of batteries up onto the stage.

"What was that?"

"Batteries."

"Why?"

"The fire alarms in this place are awfully loud, didn't want a distraction mid performance." A wicked smile leaps across his face, "Can you believe the sound system here doesn't have *We didn't start the fire* or *Burn baby burn*?" Nigel pulls a remote from his pocket and jabs a button in the direction of the light. The light switches to orange and Johnny Cash's Burning ring of fire begins filling the room from the speakers. The crazy bastard.

"You're going to set this place on fire?"

"Don't be ridiculous fire takes time to spread, I started the fire before you arrived."

The room washes red, but only for me. I feel the energy shoot through my body as my right arm swings up, fist still clenched, crashing into the side of his face, the impact knocks him to the floor. The room washes black, but not for me.

I stand shaking with adrenaline for a few seconds, sweat dripping from my brow, breathing unsteady. I can smell the smoke now, it was hard to distinguish from the musk of this place. Burning ring of fire still pounds over the speakers as I run to the doors I had come through. Locked! I shoot back in pain from the heat of the handle, no salvation beyond just a wall of flame. I run back over to the stage scouting out a fire exit I'd seen on the left of it, but Nigel had planned for this and had padlocked the doors shut. I hurry to look through the props behind the stage and find a hammer and a wrench. Rushing back to the fire door I notice the lapping orange flames have made their way into the room. I try to pull the padlock off with the wrench but it's no use, I desperately grab the hammer and begin smashing one of the handles through which the padlock is secured. The metal bends then breaks and I pull the padlock off through the gap created. Success has come just in time as I'm struggling to breathe with the smoke increase. I kick open the fire door and start running back for Nigel, I needed him to stop talking for both our sakes but I don't plan to let him die. But as I get to the front of the stage I discover I'm too late, the fire had made it's way to the fairly cheap wooden seating and the room was fully ablaze, all paths across the room were now blocked by an impenetrable wall of fire. Even the stage was alight, the curtains blazing in glory. Through the fire and smoke I can't even see Nigel across the room. I desperately look around for answers or solutions but my vision is slow and I feel dizzy. I realise time is up.

The stars dimly glow through the smoke, lanterns of the night blotted out by ash and soot. I lay on my back, staring up at the partial night sky, the shinning sentinels glowing through the smoke. The concrete of the theatre car park is icy against my back and there's a light rain, nothing significant enough to stop the hellfire.

There is peace. The sound of the theatre crackling and burning across the car park, and the distant sound of approaching sirens.

I recognize the big dipper sitting above me.

A smile grows on my face as I stare unblinking at the heavens.

The North star shines bright, undeterred by the smoke.

I feel a million small drops of rain lightly connect with my skin patterning in different spots at different times, each triggering a different nerve.

It's like a dance across my skin, neither hurts nor tickles. It's a feeling, an experience, and that makes it the most incredible thing I can ask for. Sensations so extreme had been hiding in plain sight for so long. A natural world to which a blind eye had been turned in pursuit of hollow goals. I rub my hand across the concrete beneath me and fell a hundred tiny cracks like canyons across it's surface.

The stars are disrupted by quick blue flashes as the sirens reach their destination. The smile on my face widens as I let my tired eyes rest closed.

The End

Crunching and snapping of branches bones cracking.

A thousand tiny movements. Wind thrusting through the trees, sending wild and whirling the branches.

Snap and slap in the trap.

The wind carries a presence. Dark entity without anchor in this world. A demon delving deep in the nightmarish realm of weakened minds. The shadows contort around me dancing in disguise of the entity hiding it's guise in the night.

Nightmarish realm.

In the night.

I am standing. I am aware of self. There is a blur, my world.

A twisting movement draws attention back into focus, there is

Standing nightmarish night.

A magnetic pull from the dark I feel every atom being pulled towards it. It is there. Something tall and wide.

There is burning.

My nose feels burning.

I smell burning.

Night. Sleep. Dream.

This is just a dream, I'm in a dream. Because I know this isn't possible. Can I look at my hand-------Yes that isn't my hand. My surroundings look considerably less terrifying now that they are no more than a sound stage of my mind. I look beyond the hollow trees at the writhing figure in the shadows. Claws are displayed to intimidate me. I am not afraid. My mouth is still a machine out of my reach but I'm trying desperately to extend my will there. The darkness creeps through the trees, bringing it's veil of darkness with it. Stumbling with shuffled movements I begin to see the white gleaming eyes peer through the silhouette.

This is my mouth inside of my own head. I take charge here. I do not fear you.

"What are you?"

The pearls vanish into the obsidian form as it in turn retreats into the trees.

"When-we-herd-the-way-to-survival-is-elm-many-men   -did-die-but-one-lays-down-the-path"

With these odd rasped words I'm jolted awake and drenched with a furnace inside. The familiar settings of my room calm me fairly quickly but I'm still left gasping for breath. What an odd nightmare, I guess I had managed to wake in the dream, to find realisation and power in myself. To remove any threat. I understand my dreams are my domain and I will take them back. I'll make them happy again if I have to slaughter every dark demon in them. Nothing can stop me in my dreams. I make my way out of bed, stumbling in the dark without a clue of the time. I peer down from my window at the street below, empty pavements flooded in the orange glow of the street lights. I make out one faint figure in the darkness, standing behind a car and beside a lamppost. Given the persons position out of the light and how high up I am, I can't make out any features on them. I close my curtains and head back towards my bed. I stop and look down at my hand.

4 fingers and a thumb. I'm okay now back into reality. Although now I'm ready to go back to sleep, to go into my dreams and take my power back. My eyes wander from hand across to my chest. My clean white t-shirt has a small red

speck that is enlarging exponentially. The speck becomes a full red river trickling across the untouched snow. I rip open my shirt frantically to discover a fairly deep gash across my chest leaking blood. Deep red droplets splash across the carpet , staining a deep thick red. I begin to rush for the kitchen, the first aid box, the door is gone. The door to my room I can't see it. I can't see anything. I can feel my body crumpling on the floor.

"Do not consider yourself powerful."

Printed in Great Britain
by Amazon